Sir Gibbie

George Macdonald

Edited by Kathryn Lindskoog
Illustrated by Patrick Wynne

P&R
P U B L I S H I N G
P.O.BOX 817 • PHILLIPSBURG • NEW JERSEY 08865-0817

Reprinted 2001 by P&R Publishing Co.

Printed in the United States of America

**A study guide to this edition
of *Sir Gibbie* is available
from P&R Publishing**
(1 800 631-0094)

Library of Congress Cataloging-in-Publication Data

MacDonald, George, 1862–1905.
    Sir Gibbie / George Macdonald ; edited by Kathryn Lindskoog ;
illustrated by Patrick Wynne.
        p. cm — (Classics for young readers)
    Summary: In nineteen-century Scotland, Gibbie, recently orphaned by his father's sudden death, witnesses a violent murder and flees to the coun-tryside where he finds new life and experiences many adventures.
    ISBN-10: 0-87552-726-4 (pbk.)
    ISBN-13: 978-0-87552-726-0 (pbk.)
    [1. Orphans—Fiction. 2. Adventure and adventurers—Fiction. 3. Scot-land—Social life and customs—19th century—Fiction.] I. Lindskoog, Kathryn Ann. II. Wynne, Patrick, ill. III. Title. IV. Series.

PZ7.M1475 Si 2001
[Fic]—dc21

                                                 2001034054

CONTENTS

CAST OF CHARACTERS

Gilbert (Gibbie) Galbraith—a motherless boy who can't say any words
George Galbraith—Gibbie's father, a drunken cobbler
Rev. Clement Sclater—a minister in the city
Mistress Bonniman—the fine lady who marries Mr. Sclater
Mistress Croale—the owner of a small tavern
Sambo—a kind, black sailor
Donal Grant—a young cowherd at the Mains farm
Robert Grant—Donal's father, a mountain shepherd
Janet Grant—Donal's mother
Eunice (Nicie) Grant—Donal's sister who works as a maid
John Duff—the prosperous farmer who leases the Mains of
    Glashruach
Fergus Duff—John Duff's son, a college student
Jean Mavor—John Duff's half-sister, who lives at the Mains with him
Angus MacPholp—gamekeeper at the Glashruach estate
Mistress MacPholp—the gamekeeper's wife
Thomas Galbraith—the lord of the Glashruach estate (really Mr.
    Durrant)
Ginevra (Ginny) Galbraith—motherless daughter of Thomas Galbraith
Mistress MacFarlane—Thomas Galbraith's housekeeper
Miss Kimble—a schoolmistress in the city
Mistress Murkison—Donal Grant's landlady in the city
Mr. Torrie—Rev. Sclater's lawyer in the city

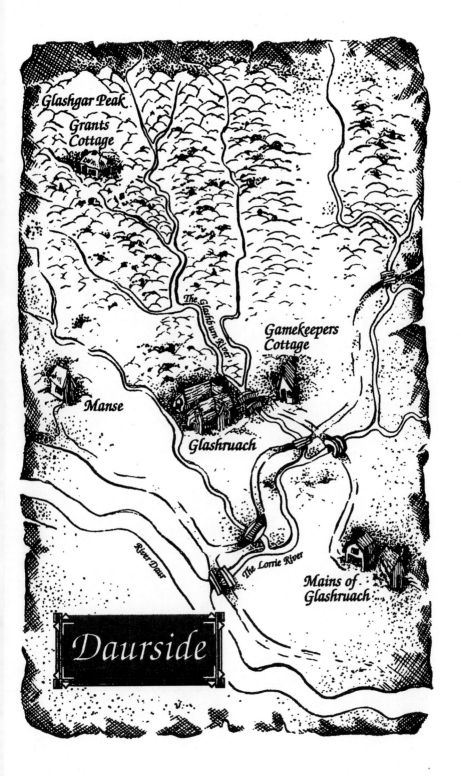

Glashgar Peak

Grants
Cottage

The Glashburn River

Gamekeepers
Cottage

Manse

Glashruach

River Daur

The Lorrie River

Mains of
Glashruach

Daurside

1

THE JEWEL IN THE GUTTER

"Come out of the gutter, you brat!"

This bellow blasted down the street from a woman with a big hole in her stocking. Her uncombed hair was tucked into a black net with wrinkled green ribbons on it for trim. Her face must have been beautiful when she was young, with her fierce dark eyes and fine straight nose. But now she was haggard.

When he heard her cry, a little boy across the street raised himself to his knees and looked at her. He had been combing the thick dirt in the gutter with his hands. He seemed only six, but he was really eight. The eyes with which he looked at her were deep blue with very long lashes, and in his lovely face they almost seemed to try to speak to her. His face was not very clever, but there was a kind of brightness in it. His hair stuck out all directions, and it would have been red-gold if the sun had not bleached it the color of hay. He stared for a moment, then returned to scraping.

Just as the woman started toward him, she heard a sharp little bell on the door of her shop announce an early customer. As the day went on toward midnight she would get more and more customers; then she would disconnect the bell on the door and stay in the parlor serving all of them whisky without stepping out again.

"The way that odd creature likes to play in the gutter! He's been

11

doing it thirty minutes!" she muttered as she poured a glass of whisky. Her early customer was so far gone with tuberculosis that he couldn't work until noon without some alcohol to relieve his misery a while, but he and the woman ignored each other.

"I would like," Mistress Croale went on to herself, "I would like for his poor father's sake—honest man!—to spank Gibbie. That liking for dirt I can't stand."

Meantime, Gibbie crept along the curb searching in the filthy mud. It was a gray autumn morning, and as the mist rose over the city at last the golden sun melted through a cloud like the slow blossoming of a flower. A ray of light brightened part of the gutter. Gibbie pounced upon what he saw there and bounded with his prize toward the sunlight. As he ran he rubbed his treasure on the little that remained of his ragged trousers. All he had to wear was an old jacket from someone three times his size and trousers that didn't reach to his knees except for a few tatters hanging down.

Gibbie held up his discovery in the sunlight and admired it. He rubbed it on his sleeve and sucked it cleaner and looked at it blissfully. It was a pretty lavender-glass earring. He ran off with it, his little bare feet sounding *thud, thud, thud* on the pavement, through street after street in the stony gray city that was his home. He never stopped trotting until he came to the door of a bakery shop:

Gibbie didn't lift the bright brass latch and go in. He stretched to peek through the window in the door into the beautiful shop. On the shelves he saw fresh loaves of bread and scones and rolls, biscuits hard and soft, and brown disks of flaky piecrust known there as buns. Best of all, he saw hot penny-loaves fresh from the oven. They looked the best to him because sometimes he did have a penny, and they were the most food he could buy for a penny anywhere. If you have never had only one penny and a great hunger you can't understand how fascinated Gibbie was, having no penny at all and only a great hunger. To him the bread smelled like paradise.

12

Gibbie knew that Missie, the baker's daughter, would soon come home from school. He had seen her crying about her lost earring that morning and was waiting to restore her earring to her. But he was so interested in all the bread that he didn't hear her approach.

"Let me in," Missie complained when she found him in her doorway. But when he handed her the earring her tone changed to appreciation.

"That's good of you, little Gibbie!" she cried. "Where did you find it?"

He pointed to the gutter, then stepped aside. She thanked him and went on in.

The baker's wife, a dull but simple and honest woman, had been dozing over her knitting and hadn't noticed Gibbie outside her door until she saw Missie arrive. "Who's that you're chatting with?" she scolded as she knit. "You mustn't be speaking to loons in the street. He's not fit company for a child like you who has a father and a mother and a bakery shop."

"Gibbie has a father, though they say he never had a mother," the girl replied.

"True, a fine father!" her mother said scornfully. "What a man to mention. Like no father at all. What did you say to Gibbie?"

"I thanked him. I lost one earring on my way to school and he found it and was here at the door to give it to me. They say he's always finding things for people."

"He's a good-hearted creature," admitted the mother. She got up and took down a penny loaf and went to the door.

"Here, Gibbie!" she cried as she opened it. "Something nice for you!"

But no Gibbie was there. He had left. She put the bread back and went on with her knitting.

2
GIBBIE'S FATHER

Even in the afternoon heat that day the shadows were chilly, but barefoot Gibbie enjoyed both sun and shadow. He enjoyed living and never felt sad about having so little. Like a little animal, he never worried about the past or future and had peace by simply enjoying whatever he could in the present. As he trotted about the city every day he was learning much about people that might make him wise when he grew older.

That day Gibbie had little to eat because he was gone when the baker's wife meant to give him a penny loaf. Luckily he found half a cookie that an angry child had thrown away. The woman who sold vegetables where Gibbie's father lived had given him a small yellow turnip, which he ate like an apple. A woman selling fish had given him all the seaweed his hands could hold; it was a kind called *dulse* that can be eaten raw. The half-cookie, the turnip, and the seaweed were all Gibbie ate that day. Gibbie got no fat out of his food, but his small body was strong and healthy. His muscles were hard, and his eyes were quick and keen. He lived in the streets like a town-sparrow.

Once Gibbie had seen a man drop his wallet and tried to slip it back into its owner's pocket secretly. The man grabbed him and was about to call the police, thinking Gibbie was surely a pick-pocket. Fortunately a young woman had seen everything and saved Gibbie. The man gave

14

Gibbie a penny as a reward, which Gibbie immediately spent on a penny loaf. No one had ever taught Gibbie to be honest. He naturally liked to restore things to their owners. When he couldn't possibly find the owner, he took what he had found home to his father. If it was worth anything, his father sold it after a few days and spent the money on whisky.

Gibbie's father George worked all day in a shed under a stairway outside what had once been a grand house for wealthy people. It was still called the Auld Hoose O' Galbraith, which is in Scotland a way to say the Old House of Galbraith. An archway was built long ago for carriages to pass under when they left the street to enter the courtyard of the huge home of the Galbraith family. The long street was now poverty stricken, and it was called Widdiehill, which means the "place of the gallows." Apparently criminals used to be hanged at the end of that street. It seemed haunted by hardship.

The great house was now divided up and many poor people rented rooms there. Gibbie's father was a cobbler who mended shoes all day in a shed in the courtyard, and awoke with a sick headache every morning in a tiny attic room up three flights of stairs. Every evening Gibbie's father spent all his day's earnings getting drunk, and every day he worked hard to earn the money to get drunk again. He did very good work and was fair to all his customers. Furthermore, he never drank alcohol unless he paid for it himself. He was an honest drunken cobbler, and that is not the worst kind of man to be. But he never even tried to take care of his only child, and he was slowly killing himself.

This forty-year-old ruin had come from rich parents and had some college education. But his own father, who had a mild alcohol problem himself, never explained family finances to George or encouraged him to prepare to earn a living. The fact was that George's father had lived on inherited wealth but had been so careless about keeping track of it that it all slipped away to other people. When

George married a fine young woman they moved into his father's ancient family home in the city where they did not have to pay rent. George's wife managed to keep him from drinking constantly. But Gibbie was born, then the young wife died, and then George's father died. The old house and everything else was sold to pay family debts that George knew nothing about, and he found himself renting a tiny room at the top of the very house that he would have inherited if his father had taken care of family affairs. George didn't inherit a penny, and he was a weak man who had never expected to have to go to work. Luckily, one of his drinking companions was a shoemaker who taught him to be a cobbler so he wouldn't starve.

Even with his drinking companions in Mistress Croale's parlor, George Galbraith was courteous, kindly, honest, and silent. At heart he had always been capable of delighting in beauty, and when he was young he had sometimes read good books and dreamed noble dreams. But the addiction that ruled his life left him only the blurs of delight and rags of colored dreams that he enjoyed every night as he escaped the real world and drank his way toward death.

How did Gibbie stay alive? There must have been poor women in the neighborhood who helped from time to time. But not one of them took any personal interest in him except for Mistress Croale. And Mistress Croale was not a tender woman.

3
AN ODD ARGUMENT

MISTRESS CROALE'S HOUSE had once belonged to her favorite aunt, and for that reason she felt obligated to keep her whisky parlor in the house respectable. She would not allow her customers to quarrel loudly; to tell dirty jokes; to swear in unusual ways; or to insult the Sabbath, the church, or the Bible. As long as they obeyed those rules and paid for their drinks, they could get as drunk as they pleased so far as she cared. As a result of her rules about respectability, she had collected a group of regular customers who were well-behaved drunkards and she rarely had any trouble with them.

Another strict rule she had was to refuse to sell to women. "No, no," she would say, "what does a woman have to do with strong drink! Let the men do as they like, we can't help *them.*" She would sell drinks to her own friends, however, and she herself had the habit of sipping whisky because of a physical ailment she spoke of often. She never said what her ailment was because there wasn't any; but she had more or less convinced herself that she had a physical excuse for using whisky as a kind of medicine. The plain fact was that she was becoming like her customers and wouldn't admit it.

She had been a church-going woman, and she still went at times. But it seemed to do more harm than good, because she got all the busier convincing herself that her way of life was blameless and guilt-free.

Maybe some of the people who turned to Jesus when he was on earth were much like Mistress Croale. She was not a bad woman, but she was slowly and surely growing worse. Her conscience was uneasy.

On the morning when Gibbie found the lost earring, she was replacing the black bottle on the shelf when the door opened again.

"What do you want?" she asked without turning around.

The silence made her turn to look. There stood a man in a dark suit with a white collar, glaring at her with disapproval. It was the new minister of the local parish, Reverend Clement Sclater.

"What do you want, sir?" she asked with more respect but less friendliness than before.

"I want you to shut up this whisky shop and find yourself a more decent way of life in my parish," he answered pompously.

"Allow me to tell you, sir," she snapped furiously, "you're the first that ever dared say my house is not decent."

For a moment they argued about whether her house was decent or not if the parlor of the house was a whisky shop. Mistress Croale compared her nice clean house to other whisky shops in the neighborhood.

"I give you fair warning," he answered, "that I mean to do what I can to shut up all the whisky shops in my parish." This alarmed her. The minister did not rule the section of the city where his church was, but he might be able to persuade city officials to refuse to renew her whisky license.

"It's a real pity, doubtless," she said in a softer tone, "that there should be so many thirsty throats in the kingdom, sir. But thirst must drink, and you know, sir, if it is withheld from them, many would cut their throats."

"They're cutting their throats in the long run anyway," he answered.

"But as long as there's whisky," she answered quickly, "it will take the throat-road. It's the nature of whisky to run down throats, and there's no going against nature. If the thing must be, you'll have to admit—

18

and I'm telling you the truth—that it's no small benefit to the town that the drunken creatures fill themselves decently—and that's what I see to. Sir, I'm like a mother to the poor men. If you learn that there is ever any disorder or immorality in my shop, I'll close it in a minute. But if you drive my customers to other whisky shops you'll just make them far worse than they are."

"But Mistress Croale," Mr. Sclater answered in a religious tone, "it's not only your drunken customers I want to help. Your soul is as precious to me as any in the parish."

"As precious as Mistress Bonniman's?" she shot back. She had heard that this new minister was much attracted to the rich and beautiful young widow Mrs. Bonniman. A shadow of embarrassment crossed his face.

"No, no, sir!" she hurried on. "Whatever value my soul has to my Maker, don't pretend that it's of value in your eyes like the soul of such a fine, pretty, charming young lady. I haven't had such an easy life, and maybe I'll be judged a bit easier than some fine folk."

"I wouldn't count on that," Mr. Sclater advised. He felt safer warning sinners about hell than talking about the lovely Mrs. Bonniman.

At that Mistress Croale launched into a magnificent speech about all her own virtues from cleanliness and strict Sabbath observance and church offerings, to never-ever inviting anyone to drink whisky. "I would have no man's death, soul or body, lie at my door." She admitted that her one fault was that she didn't read the Bible so often as she should, and then she thanked Mr. Sclater for caring enough to come to look after her because the previous minister had never come to see her once in all his time in the parish although she donated to the church. She practically turned their conversation inside-out.

"Well, well," Mr. Sclater answered in a daze. "I don't doubt a word of what you tell me; but you know works cannot save us. Our best righteousness is but as filthy rags." He sensed that this answer didn't fit the situation at all, but he was at a loss.

"How well I know that Scripture, Mr. Sclater. And I'll be glad to see you any time you do me the favor to look in as you pass by. It's no disgrace, sir, for mine's an honest business in a clean house."

"I'll do that, Mistress Croale," he answered, glad to escape. "But please remember what I said." He left before she could answer.

She immediately took the bottle back down and drank a glass of whisky. His visit had made her start trembling. Then the whisky made her feel bad and she vowed never to take it again. It can seem easy to quit drinking right after a drink. But when the thirst arises one drinks again. Mistress Croale set about her housework with a sad sigh. It would not have comforted her any if she had realized that her clever tongue had defended whisky shops more skillfully than the rich owners of the whisky industry could have done. She always tried to convince herself that she really was a very good woman. That was her mistake. Mr. Sclater's mistake was that he didn't even need convincing that he was a very good man; he was sure of it. He did not yet realize that he was proud of himself and didn't understand people.

Only time could show if either Mistress Croale or Mr. Sclater would turn out right. And Gibbie, who had just danced away with the earring outside, would make all the difference.

4
ONE SATURDAY NIGHT

AFTER MR. SCLATER LEFT Mistress Croale's parlor, the autumn day went on and on and went out, quenched in chilly fog. All along Widdiehill gas lights were turned on in dingy shops. In his shed, George Galbraith had lit a candle in order to keep at work as long as the street was light. With great relief, he blew out the candle and locked the shed as soon as dark had fallen, heading straight for his earthly paradise. Like all of Mistress Croale's customers, he walked to her place without running and stumbling and tried to hide his great hurry. Her customers strolled along trying to look as if they were going somewhere for tea and as if they felt fine.

"There's his own worst enemy," said the vegetable woman kindly as he passed her door.

"Yes," said a neighbor, "but to see that poor neglected baby of his scouring about the town with a few rags on. If his mother could see him she would turn over in her grave. It makes a mother's heart sick to see him."

George reached Mistress Croale's first that night. The room was clean and cheerful, lit by a busy little fire in the grate. A kettle of hot water was already crooning, ready for making toddy drinks. The black bottle and glasses were waiting on the table. Mistress Croale was extra neat and nicely dressed, waiting for her customers.

"Welcome, Sir George," she said. "But you must have forgotten that this is Saturday night. You might not get up early enough to get shaved before church in the morning." She knew he never went to church, but she often talked as if everyone went. Sir George was used to it.

"True, I had forgotten," he said, rubbing his whiskers. "I wish I had put on a clean shirt and washed my face. I'll go over to the barber shop for a shave and come right back." Mistress Croale knew perfectly well that he owned only one shirt, but she appreciated courteous talk like this. She liked George Galbraith. She had given him this very shirt from those left when her husband died.

In a few minutes George returned with the lower half of his face smooth and clean. Because he had no mirror or razor of his own, he needed to go to a barber shop more often than he did. He rarely even washed himself. Mistress Croale sent him upstairs to wash his hands and the rest of his face and to put on a clean shirt that had been her husband's. George's whole soul was craving alcohol, but he obeyed Mistress Croale politely. By the time he returned to the parlor to drink, his companions were there also.

Mistress Croale didn't care about any of her customers except Sir George. She was sorry that he was a heavy drinker and a bad father, but she was glad that he drank in her safe sheepfold instead of some disgusting pig sty. She really considered her shop a haven for decent drinkers.

As they measured out their whisky and stirred sugar and hot water into it for their toddies, the men grew merrier and merrier. But Sir George (and "Sir" was his inherited title as a baronet—a minor nobleman) stared into his glass and only smiled to be polite. Alcohol helped him to imagine that he was a person of high rank. The shave and clean shirt made him long for a better life. But he felt he could no more live without drinking whisky than without breathing air.

22

5
GIBBIE'S SECRET LIFE

LIKE A MOTH FLYING AROUND A LAMP, Gibbie spent six nights a week
trotting around outside Mistress Croale's parlor. He could run backward almost as fast as forward, from much practice. He would stand
and listen under the window where light shone through a red curtain,
then dart off like a bird and trot up and down the street, then return.
He did this twenty or even a hundred times in an evening. While his
father floated inside in warm dreams about being a rich man, poor little Gibbie was waiting out in the frosty dark of the autumn night. He
was waiting to take his father home.

This evening near midnight he heard his father's own voice for a
change. The voice Gibbie loved said "Up Daurside!" The words meant
nothing to Gibbie, but they were fixed in his brain because his father
had said them. Soon Mistress Croale announced that it was closing
time because she refused to break Sabbath by letting the men stay
after midnight on Saturday night. They bumped and stumbled to the
door obediently, too far gone to say good night. Last out and most
drunk, as usual, was Gibbie's father. Mistress Croale watched until
Gibbie darted out of the darkness to help him.

For a year and a half Sir George had never slept in the gutter at
night because Gibbie had figured out how to get his father home safely.

If you can imagine a very small boy trying to prop up a very tall man who reeled and staggered in every direction, you can get an idea of what Gibbie accomplished. He had to dance around his father like a tiny prize-fighter, his feet barely touching the ground. His skill and speed and judgment were those of an athlete, and his purpose was that of a guardian angel. The hardest part for Gibbie was getting his unconscious father up three flights of stairs. Then it was easy to steer him to their only piece of furniture, a rickety bed, where George could collapse.

Then came the happiest moments of Gibbie's day. He spread over his sleeping father his dead mother's tartan plaid blanket and nestled against his father's chest, which was paradise to Gibbie. For a few dark hours his father could not leave him and the two would be together again. Sir George never knew it, of course, and Gibbie could only stay awake to enjoy it a few minutes before he fell asleep. But for him those few minutes made every day a victory. Gibbie clung to his one possession, his father, who was all in all to him.

6

A SUNDAY AT HOME

SUNDAY WAS THE HAPPIEST DAY of the week for Gibbie. It was the day when his father stayed in their tiny room with him with a hangover.

This Sunday Gibbie lay awake blissfully close to his father under the plaid blanket. Finally his father awoke and pushed Gibbie away. Unable to walk, the man crawled across the room and pulled himself to an empty chest where he sat in misery for half an hour. Gibbie looked on like one awaiting a resurrection. And finally a slight resurrection came.

There was no mention of breakfast. There never was. George picked up a little half-made shoe and Gibbie clapped with delight. For as long as he could remember, Gibbie had spent Sundays waiting for his father to make him a pair of shoes. Gibbie had never had any shoes in his life except for the pair of little wool baby socks that his mother had put on him when he was a tiny baby before she died. Today was the day when his father was going to finish the second shoe in the pair that he was making for Gibbie. The boy could hardly contain his joy, but he knew that he must be soft as a shadow because his father's head hurt. And he always felt that he mustn't hug his father unless the man was drunk and didn't know it. So he watched closely and sometimes danced silently behind the sick cobbler.

Incredible as it seems, Sir George was trying to think of some

Christian teaching for his son. George wouldn't consider going to church, and Gibbie didn't even know what church was for. But George had been taught something of Christianity as a child. He knew that although some people considered Gibbie an idiot, the boy could learn. For several years George had planned to buy a book and teach Gibbie about God, but he never got it done. Now he tried to recall something about God from his muddled memory. He had a vague fear that Gibbie might go to hell if he didn't learn about God. After brooding over this for a long time he managed to recall one sentence from his own Christian education: "Man's chief end is to glorify God, and to enjoy him forever." As he worked on the little shoe, George simply repeated that empty sentence dozens of times while all he thought about was how badly he wanted some whisky.

Gibbie listened closely and memorized the words without being asked to do so. He thought his father said, "Man's *chiefenn* is to glorify God, and to enjoy him forever," and it was years before he learned what the sentence meant. But he liked it.

When George thought that Gibbie had probably learned the sentence, he felt somehow better than he had felt in years. Then he sent Gibbie to Mistress Croale's to pick up some cooked beef and broth and potatoes that he had paid for Saturday evening.

Every Sunday afternoon father and son ate their one meal of the week together this way, without a table. Gibbie's joy was somewhat spoiled by the fact that he worried because his father ate so little. George had no appetite any more for food, only for whisky.

Mistress Croale's conscience would not allow her to sell drinks on Sunday. Furthermore, George's conscience would not allow him to work for pay on Sunday or to drink whisky until evening on any day. That made Sunday afternoons miserably long for George and is why he worked on shoes for Gibbie until whisky hours arrived. The fact is that he always felt less guilty about his life because he spent Sundays making shoes for his son, although his son was eight years old and

26

many Sundays had passed indeed, and still no shoes.

At last the second little shoe was done and Gibbie was breathless with delight. But for the fourth time George had made Gibbie a pair of shoes too small for his little feet. George seemed as sunk in despair as Gibbie. As usual, he made the shoes too small for his own son and sold them to a shoe store where parents would buy them for other children. George always spent the shoe money on whisky, and Gibbie never got a pair of shoes. Neither father nor son suspected that this habit was partly intentional. Gibbie was too innocent to suspect that, and George was too hazy.

When Gibbie roused from his grief enough to see his father sitting slumped on the edge of the bed in dejection, he bounded to him and embraced him with his little arms. He only dared to do it because he so wanted to comfort the poor man. Sir George got tears in his dull eyes, and kissed Gibbie for perhaps the first time. Then he measured Gibbie's feet on brown paper as he had done before in order to start the long process again next Sunday. But blessed darkness had come at last and George felt free to start drinking.

"Go to visit Mistress Croale, Gibbie," he said as usual at this time on Sunday. He didn't like to uncork his Sunday bottle while Gibbie watched. Mistress Croale expected Gibbie and gave him skim milk and all the stale bread he wanted. She sat and had tea and buttered toast while he stood and ate stale bread, and they both thought she was kind and generous. He looked at her with loving, grateful eyes. She fought down her fear that she was Gibbie's enemy and kept busy convincing herself that she really helped him and his father.

When Gibbie got home his father was busy drinking and had come alive.

"Gibbie," he said as he gulped from his mug, "never drink a drop of whisky! It's been the curse of the Galbraiths as far back as I know. Never drink anything but water! Don't do it."

Gibbie shook his head obediently.

"Do you know what they'll call you when I'm dead? They'll call you Sir Gibbie Galbraith, my man. You'll have the honor of the family to hold up." Sir George rambled on more and sent Gibbie to bed.

Half an hour later Gibbie saw his father jump up looking very pale and then kneel down and pour out a long prayer of misery to God. He explained to God that he was not a drunkard, only a problem drinker and a victim of whisky. He begged for help. He confessed that he could not even pray without a drink or two to get him started. He begged to be saved from evil.

Gibbie had never heard his father pray before. Although the prayer was one of a tormented man, it soothed Gibbie so that when his father fell forward on the bed groaning and then fell silent, Gibbie went to sleep.

Later Gibbie awakened and couldn't get his father up onto the bed. So he eased him to the floor and made a bed and slept next to him there. Later still, Gibbie awakened very cold and thought his father's face looked very strange in the moonlight. The face felt cold. Gibbie, who knew nothing about death, tried and tried to awaken his father. Finally he realized that his father was not breathing. He lifted one of his father's eyelids and screamed in despair. It was the scream of an orphan.

7
THE CITY ORPHAN

SOME WOULD THINK THAT GIBBIE would get along better after the loss of such a father; but it was not so. To him the streets and the people and the shops, even the penny-loaves, lost half their delight when his father was no longer in the background. To Gibbie his father had been the heart of the happy city. But life was still life to Gibbie, and he ran about as before. He roamed the streets all day and part of the night as usual; he took what was given to him and picked up what he found.

Not one of the poor women who now and then gave Gibbie a penny or a bit of bread or a scrap of meat or a pair of old trousers felt the poorer for the gift. He accepted kindness and passed it on, caring little more about the details than a kitten cares if its milk comes in a white saucer or a blue saucer. Kindness was the main part of any gift.

A group of women in Mr. Sclater's congregation felt that they should rescue Gibbie and civilize him. They collected money to board him for a year with a cranky old woman who taught school. He spent one night in her house, and she started to teach him the next morning. When he reached up to stroke her unfriendly face in gratitude as she leaned over him, she pushed him away and lifted her cane to punish him for the insult. Right then her other pupils were unhappily blundering through the twenty-third psalm. Gibbie forever thought of "thy rod and thy staff" as tools for beating students rather than tools for protecting them. He bolted out the door, ran far away, and never set foot on that woman's street again. So he lost his first chance at education.

No one knew exactly where Gibbie slept.

In the summer he slept anywhere, and in winter he slept where he could find warmth. Sometimes he slept by the furnace of the steam-engine of the water-works. The police would have laughed at the idea of taking him in if anyone had complained that he was a tramp. They knew about him. It takes either wisdom or plenty of experience to know that a child is not necessarily wicked even if brought up in far worse circumstances than Gibbie's.

The police knew that Gibbie was utterly harmless and that he had a knack for finding things for people. Gibbie followed the town crier who beat a drum and announced what was lost and found. He often brought the crier things he had found, and the crier encouraged him to keep at it but never paid him at all. Once in a while he gave Gibbie a penny, as if out of kindness. The truth was that he owed Gibbie many pennies indeed; but Gibbie never realized that people paid the crier for Gibbie's findings. And, to tell the truth, he wouldn't have cared. It never occurred to Gibbie that life could be or would be fair. He had no idea of justice.

The police also knew that Gibbie spent many hours each night playing guardian angel to drunkards. The police claimed that Gibbie came to know every one of them in the city, where the person lived, and where the person usually got drunk as well. They did not know that he did this out of love for his dead father; they assumed that he did it because he was a bit crazy. But it was certainly helpful to them.

Of course Gibbie was least known to those he helped the most. He never received any thanks for his kindness, and sometimes he received blows and abuse. But he was good at dodging blows as he propped up the staggering hulks and prodded them homeward.

Usually people showed Gibbie no gratitude for his good deeds, but he had never been taught to expect any or even to wish for any. Sometimes he helped his father's old companions, but nothing could entice him to go near Mistress Croale's house itself because of his strong memories of his father there.

8

A MAN CALLED SAMBO

No ONE WAS SORRIER about Sir George's death or said more kind words about him than Mistress Croale. She seemed to be fighting the suspicion in her heart that she had been partly to blame. She wanted to soothe her conscience by being kinder to Gibbie, but she couldn't do it because he wouldn't come near her house. It was obvious that after Sir George's death Mistress Croale went downhill fast. She not only drank more in private, but drank with her customers and forgot the house rules that she had taken such pride in.

As soon as her whisky shop lost its good reputation, Mr. Sclater got the help of her unhappy neighbors and had her license revoked. She simply sold her house and bought a worse one on the river-bank, far from Mr. Sclater's church parish. She had no more license to sell whisky and pretended to rent out rooms instead. But in fact the sailors and river workers who came there every night found plenty to drink along with all kinds of excitement such as gambling and fighting. Mistress Croale no longer seemed nice enough to be called Mistress; all her new customers called her Lucky Croale. She was breaking the law and they all knew it.

In the second winter after his father's death, when Gibbie was nine, he ran into Lucky Croale on the street one day. He was happy to see her, and he visited her new home often. She welcomed him. He was shocked to hear her use language that she wouldn't allow her customers to use in the old days, but he always took things as he found them without much question. He disliked ugliness, but he didn't fret about it. He enjoyed the jolly ways and open-hearted kindness of many of the sailors who came to her shop, and most of them liked him.

Gradually, Gibbie spent less and less time at night guiding drunkards home and spent more time at the Croale house protecting drunken men there. They were forever quarreling, and almost every night he entered a fight before it got bad and tried to make peace between the rough men. He often succeeded, because he had an instinct for helping people. He saw bad things there, but evil was only an unfortunate fact to Gibbie, and that was all. It didn't really interest him. His face and eyes sometimes seemed to show keen intelligence, but usually they just showed the happy innocence of a much younger child.

That such a boy should exist was, of course, unlikely. Such a person is rare. But that does not make such a person impossible or subhuman. It is the most noble person who is most human. Gibbie was a rarity, but a rarity very precious to the human race. Gibbie had a talent for loving people. He loved human faces and human voices far more than most of us do. That is what kept him pure and honest and busy. He was as overflowing with love as some other rare child genius is overflowing with music.

In the spring Gibbie met a black sailor who rented a room at Lucky Croale's while waiting for his next ship. He was nicknamed Sambo by the other men; so Sambo he was called. Gibbie approached him right away because he liked the shining dark eyes and flashing smile. Sambo soon loved Gibbie tenderly, and they were devoted friends. Although Sambo was immensely strong, he tolerated almost any amount of rudeness and mistreatment from crude light-skinned people. He had self-control.

In one rush he knocked down all the cardplayers with the table,
causing bottles and glasses to fall on top of them.

One night as Gibbie was nestled on Sambo's lap, Sambo happened to laugh, being a good-humored man, at something in the card game that was going on in the room. A sailor from Malaysia, who was losing, got furious and cursed Sambo. Then the others all decided that Sambo had to join their card game, probably intending to cheat him and start a fight. Sambo simply refused to play cards no matter how they yelled at him. They weren't used to being disobeyed by a black man. One heaved a heavy drinking glass at Sambo and it hit Gibbie on the head before Sambo could protect him. In a mad rage, he set Gibbie down gently in the corner and then in one rush knocked down all the cardplayers with the table, causing bottles and glasses to fall on top of them.

Seeing what he had done, he lifted the table up to free them, laughed at his foolishness, and carried Gibbie upstairs. Gibbie went to sleep on the way in Sambo's arms.

Hours later Gibbie awakened on a cot in a large closet, missing his father and imagining his father's death again. He opened the door and looked into Sambo's bedroom. Several men were quietly struggling until there was the sound of a great gush. The men fled.

"O Lord Jesus!" Sambo moaned. They were his last words. The men had bent his head back as he slept and gashed his neck open. Gibbie stood frozen in terror.

All he could recall after that was running like the wind in the streets. The next morning he found himself on the high bridge over the river Daur that led out of the city he had always loved, his only home. Now he feared the city because he had finally seen evil for what it is, and he knew that Sambo couldn't breathe any more and couldn't say a word and would have to be buried as his father had been buried. Gibbie recalled the night he had heard his father say "Up Daurside!" That was the direction he was headed. He decided to go on far, far away from the gaping hole in Sambo's big throat.

Down in the city Lucky Croale called the police and the murderers were soon caught and eventually executed. But the fact came out that the last time anyone saw Gibbie he was in the arms of Sambo on his way upstairs before the murder. The news spread, and the whole city was in a commotion for fear that the murderers had killed Gibbie also. Alive or dead, he was sought everywhere in the city. The killers said, of course, that they hadn't touched him. But their words meant nothing because they had slit the throat of an innocent man.

There was so much talk about Gibbie that Mr. Sclater decided to try to get the boy's history straight. He did some investigating. He found that if Gibbie was alive he was in fact Sir Gilbert Galbraith, Baronet, but that the family fortune had all been lost. Some of the mother's relatives were alive, but they had disowned her for marrying George Galbraith and didn't care that she died and left a little son. In a storage area next to the room where Sir George had died, Mr. Sclater discovered a box of Galbraith family papers which at least proved what he had already learned. Most were very old property deeds.

Being a careful man, Mr. Sclater took the box home and stored it in the attic of the church manse where he lived. The papers might be of sentimental value to descendants of the family some day if any were alive. Unfortunately, there was not much hope in the city that Sir Gilbert, everyone's little Gibbie, could be alive any more. He was gone.

9

THE RUNAWAY

FOR THE FIRST TIME IN HIS LIFE, the fatherless, motherless, brotherless, sisterless stray of the streets felt alone. That gash in Sambo's black throat had killed the whole city for him. People were the world to him, and in his shock he felt that the human face was what he could no longer look upon. That one black face with the white, staring eyes, the cruel new mouth in its throat, and the white grinning teeth haunted him. Gibbie's sweet face had usually protected him from hurt; he was brave and hardy. He was not afraid for his safety. And he was not shocked most by the hideous loss of his friend. He was shocked most by the failure of his confidence in his own love for others. He had recoiled. That jarred him out of every groove of thought, every socket of habit, every joint of action. He was cast from the city as a wanderer in strange surroundings, but also in a strange inner world.

It was a cold fresh morning in April when Gibbie began his journey up the side of the Daur river. Sparkles of rain, the smell of damp earth, farm fields, wildflowers— these were new to Gibbie but of no interest at all. To him the countryside was no beautiful discovery; it was emptiness. If he passed someone on the road he felt stared at in an unfriendly way; in fact, he didn't know how strange he looked to them. Soon he hid when he saw someone coming. His tough feet got sore from sharp stones in the road and he had to slow to a walk. He was very hungry.

At last Gibbie spied a field of small yellow turnips and gathered all he could carry. In the city vegetable owners stayed with their merchandise. Here he saw no owner, and so he thought the turnips were free. Here everything looked lost and ownerless to Gibbie. As he walked along gobbling turnips like a rabbit, a little girl by the roadside saw him and offered him an oatmeal pancake. He accepted it gladly and offered her a turnip, which she refused scornfully. Gibbie soon came to a stream, which he considered dirty like gutter water in the city. But it was so sparkling that he decided to try it and found that it was delicious clean water.

It was a cold day, and as dusk settled Gibbie felt a fear of the dark for the first time in his life. Fortunately, he came to a farmyard where he could look for a place to sleep warmer than the road. He discovered an empty shed for a dog and crawled under some straw and fell fast asleep.

Soon the Newfoundland dog returned and was fastened to his chain for the night by the boy who owned him. The boy couldn't see Gibbie and left. Knowing that the dog might attack him for trespassing, Gibbie tried a run for the door in vain. The dog was too fast. So Gibbie started to bark in a friendly way. The dog was startled. Then Gibbie laughed and they became friends at once. Humans had failed him, but here was a dog. They played and then curled up to sleep together, full of affection. Then supper came for the dog, a bowl of porridge and milk. Gibbie didn't get much, scooping with his hand while the dog gobbled it down, but it was his best food of the day. After that the two slept in a tangle of arms and legs until sunrise.

Gibbie set the dog free to romp and went on his way. A band of Gypsies met him that day and fed him from their kettle. They knew he would be a good beggar for them to train. But he was suspicious because of the look in their eyes and sneaked away from the tent at night and hurried on his way. He was no longer purely trusting.

So every day Gibbie survived one way or another. A weaker child would have died from cold and hunger. His habit of moving fast all the time, learned in cold city streets, helped to save him in the cold countryside. Food was scarce, but he kept from starving. Drink was to be had at any stream. Sleep was scattered all over the world.

10

THE STRANGE BARN

It was May, but up in the hills where Gibbie traveled May sometimes shook from her skirts flurries of snow or hail, as if she were really April or March. Then the sun would shine a bit as if to say, "I could not stop that ice, but I'm up here all the same, bringing summer as fast as I can!"

Gibbie felt as if he had been on his journey for months, but it had only been a few weeks. Not once since he set out had he had a chance to do anything for anybody; and for Gibbie not being able to help others was like being dead or imprisoned. He passed farm after farm, of course, but he thought that country people are unfriendly. He did not realize that they simply did not know who he was; and back where he came from most people had known. So people who passed him on the road looked at him with curiosity that he failed to understand.

Lacking people, Gibbie began to turn his love to nature. When he started his journey he was so sad and stunned that the new sights and smells meant nothing to him. But now, one daisy was enough to delight him, and in sheltered places he saw whole patches of wildflowers. He no longer feared the Daur river. Sometimes he lay for hours listening to it murmur over its pebbly bed. He saw sheep grazing on the hillsides between clumps of heather, and now spring lambs were frolicking.

Best of all, for Gibbie, was the wind. In the city he had hardly noticed it, but now it was his friend. When he was hot from walking it cooled him and brought him sweet country smells. Even when it was cold he liked it because it seemed alive and touched him. It seemed to love him and kiss him on the forehead. Except for one sad moment on the day his father died, Gibbie did not remember having been kissed by human beings. Where he grew up women didn't even kiss their own children very much. So not one of them ever thought of kissing this beggar child. His father never thought of it until his dying day. So it was the May wind in the hills that slowly taught Gibbie to enjoy soft touches.

One evening, he discovered a field of clover beyond a rough gate and thought it would make a good bed. He had never had a cold in his life, so sleeping in the open didn't hurt him. It had never crossed his mind that he might ever get sick. He was very hungry, but he was used to that. He lay down and went right to sleep as usual.

Later he awakened from hunger in bright moonlight. Nearby he saw twenty or thirty large round hay ricks, which are like very neat, solidly-constructed haystacks. Gibbie had seen many of these in the distance and guessed that they were somehow for the benefit of cows and horses, who seemed to like hay. Gibbie assumed that country people took care of cows and horses simply in order to keep the animals comfortable and happy. He suspected that the countryside was made for cattle and the city was made for people. That would explain why country people didn't know how to act like real people. The few times he had ventured into farmyards he had been told to get out and go away. Not one person had greeted him in the country.

Because the wind turned cold, Gibbie wandered among the ricks for some protection; how huge they seemed. Then Gibbie discovered a long low building nearby. The door was locked, but at the bottom there was a little special door for cats. In fact, Gibbie had discovered a very old-fashioned barn. Farmers want cats to catch the mice and rats that eat the grain in the barn. Cats aren't tempted to eat the grain. But you can be sure that farmers don't put cat doors in their dairies, because cats steal milk as eagerly as rats steal grain. Gibbie knew nothing at all about any of this. He just felt cold and sleepy and somehow managed to squeeze inside through the cat door. He burrowed into a heap of golden straw in the moonlight and sank into soft warm sleep.

What awakened Gibbie in the morning was the sound of very heavy blows. He peered out through the straw and thought he saw the body of an old man on the floor, and two men beating him to death with large sticks. Gibbie was paralyzed with horror. Perhaps he was still half-asleep, and perhaps he had been dreaming about the murder of Sambo. Gradually Gibbie's old man faded away and in his place Gibbie saw clearly a heap of straw. He watched the workmen throw down another sheaf and beat the grain out of it, then toss the straw on the heap where he was hiding. Luckily the man with the pitchfork didn't see Gibbie's eyes peeking out or he might have mistaken him for a little wild animal and plunged the pitchfork into him!

After over an hour of pounding, the men left. Gibbie was very hungry and guessed they went to breakfast. He crept out and tried a mouthful of raw oats, husks and all. They were impossible to chew. Next Gibbie found the hayloft and climbed up. Under the rafters a row of big round cheeses were stored on a shelf to ripen with age. Gibbie had seen cheese in shops in the city and knew they were good food, although he assumed they grew in the fields like turnips.

Gibbie still had the idea that things in the country belong to nobody in particular and were mostly for the use of animals. He didn't suspect that the cheese belonged to someone who had made it and wanted to keep it. He also didn't suspect that some cheese has a tough rind on the outside that is usually cut off. He pounced upon a cheese and lifted it with both hands and began nibbling. To his delight he found the softer part inside. But just then the workers returned to the barn and Gibbie lay down flat to hide.

One reason Gibbie feared the men's sticks was what he had seen on the road a few days before. He had discovered a little hedgehog as he walked along and was admiring its wonderful stiff hair like great pins. Just then the driver of a cart noticed the little hedgehog and killed it with one blow with his whip as he rode by. Gibbie felt the whole world must be full of killing.

Finally thirst forced Gibbie to squirm along to explore the loft, and to his amazement he found himself in a stable. Several horses were eating hay. Gibbie tried some and choked on it and coughed. How could horses eat it? Apparently the cheese on the shelf was for the horses also. One of the horses was beautiful and white, and he would have enjoyed feeding it a piece of cheese.

Just then a man came in and led two horses away. He left the stable door open. Gibbie ran out and headed across the field toward a low area with trees—a hollow—where he would probably find water.

11
FINDING JANET

WHEN HE LIFTED HIS HEAD from drinking at the stream, he was curious about where the stream came from. As he trotted along, he saw that this way up the stream would lead him too far from the Daur river, but he found a very small stream that he decided to follow instead. He sped happily past pine forest and fresh spring larch trees. He came to a bridge where an iron gate stood between stone pillars with a stone wolf's head at the top of each. Inside he saw a tame white rabbit that had escaped from its hutch. Suddenly a large spaniel came to attack it. Gibbie shrieked, and the two bounded into the woods out of sight. Gibbie turned away sadly.

"Each strong creature," he thought, "hurts weak creatures." It was his first conscious thought about how life goes. Within a few years he would add to it, "But the person who is really human breaks that rule."

Gibbie kept going long after his trot turned into a difficult hike. He was still seeking the origin of the little stream.

Gibbie never thought about his looks at all. The fact is that his trousers were shapeless rags. He had never had a shirt in his life and still wore the old jacket that was huge on him. He folded back the long sleeves clear to his elbows and used that inner space for carrying things. His legs and feet were bare, as always, and his head was covered with a wild crown of sunbleached hair that stuck out all over as if it were electrified. His wild hair was a great contrast to his peaceful face. The peace of Gibbie's face looked alive, his features were well-shaped, and his eyes were large and soft. Sometimes his eyes looked sharply alert. And always it seemed as if something behind them was waiting to wake up. His whole small body was well put together, but his clothes disguised that fact.

This is how Gibbie looked when he arrived at the highest home on the mountain. It was a wonderful little old cottage built on stone, with a straw roof, nestled among giant rocks. A good cow lived outside the cottage in the protection of a projecting rock. A poor couple who had grown too old for farm life had recently moved to this old cottage. Gibbie automatically knocked on the weatherbeaten door.

"Come on in, whoever you are." The voice was rich and lively.

Gibbie entered and saw a small woman with gray hair and clear gray eyes dressed all in blue with a frilly white cap on her head, resting on a stool with a book on her lap.

"Oh, you poor outcast! How did you come way up here? You have left the world behind you. What would you like? I have nothing."

Gibbie only smiled.

The fact is that Janet had been reading these words of Jesus in her Bible just before Gibbie knocked: "Inasmuch as ye have done it to the least of these, my brethren, ye have done it unto me." With her heart full of these words she looked at Gibbie and thought for a moment that he was Jesus come to her as a boy. There stood the child, and whether he was the Lord or not, he was evidently hungry. And perhaps the Lord is hungry in every hungry child.

As Gibbie looked at her innocently her awe deepened. She made him sit on her stool while she took a platter of oatcakes from a hole in the wall and put them on her clean white table. She carried a wooden bowl out to her dairy in the cool rock and brought it back filled with creamy milk. Then she put a chair at the table.

"Sit down and eat. If you were the Lord himself, and you may be for all I know, for you look pure and neglected enough, I could give no better, for it's all I have to offer you—unless I might have an egg." She hurried out.

She came back with two eggs, which she buried in the hot ashes of her peat fire to roast while Gibbie ate the hearty oatcake and drank mountain milk such as most boys could never imagine, it was so good. Janet sat on her stool knitting so that Gibbie wouldn't feel hurried. She kept glancing up at him, and he said nothing and her sense of mystery grew.

Suddenly the door flew open and a splendid collie came in and dropped a tiny half-dead lamb in Janet's lap. It was a good sheep dog indeed. The mother sheep had been sold and sent away, but she had escaped and come a great distance to give birth to her lamb on this mountain. "Mba-a" she said as she trotted in and went to Janet for help. Her udder was full of milk, but her lamb was too weak to suck.

Janet carried the lamb to her bed at the side of the room and covered it. Then she milked the mother a little and took the milk to the lamb. Gibbie couldn't see how she fed the milk to the lamb, but his busy eyes and loving heart took in all the rest. Meanwhile, Oscar the collie welcomed Gibbie by staring at him and now and then licking his little brown feet.

Gibbie always ate so fast that he finished quickly. He gratefully left the cottage in silence. When Janet turned away from the lamb she saw Oscar looking at the empty chair.

She asked Oscar where the boy went, as if the dog were to blame, and rushed to the door; but Gibbie had already disappeared up the mountainside. Now Janet had to bake more oatcakes for her husband. That was simple, but it was painful because her joints ached with rheumatism. This was the last oatmeal until her grown son should carry up a bag next Saturday; but that didn't matter much. It is added pain that is the hardest part of hospitality, harder than running out of food.

Finally all her work was done again and she sat back down with her Bible. The lamb lay at her feet and she felt as if somehow the lamb was the boy who had fed there. After she had read awhile she felt as if the lamb was the Lord himself, both lamb and shepherd, come to her house. Then for fear that she had too much imagination, she knelt down and prayed.

Janet hadn't been to church for years because she couldn't walk that far from the farm. She had no book but the Bible and no help to understand it but the highest help of all, and her faith was simple and strong. Day by day she studied the first four books of the New Testament and came to know Jesus as he is. That meant that she obeyed him. To Janet Jesus Christ was a living man who somehow or other heard her when she called him and sent her the help she needed.

12

GLASHGAR PEAK

GIBBIE CLIMBED AND CLIMBED, even when the path went no farther and he had lost his little stream. All below and around him was red granite rock. He came to the absolute top of Glashgar peak, which was only about three thousand feet in height, but very steep. Gibbie was disappointed at first when he saw that in every direction the slope was downward. He had never been on top of anything before.

He sat down and gazed at distant mountains and gazed more and dreamed. Above was infinite blue sky, with the sun heading west. It was as if Gibbie had climbed to the throne of the world. And from unknown fountains the heart of the lonely child filled at last. In later years when Gibbie had learned to think about God and desire his presence and believe in his love, this moment of silence on the top of Glashgar peak was the feeling in his heart.

Now a strange thing happened. In very little time he was surrounded by a storm cloud that hid everything. There was a deafening crack and roar and roll of thunder with brilliant light in the cloud around him, and wind that almost blew him away. He clung to the rock, in the center of a tempest. Water poured down the mountainsides. Gibbie thought this was all wonderful. As soon as it was safe, he jumped up and danced in the rain. Then the storm stopped and water ran on down the mountain and the sun was shining again as it slipped down the western sky.

Gibbie intended to find a dry hole and sleep as close to the kindly cottage as possible. He had never accepted favors from the same house twice in one day, so he did not think of knocking at the door again. But he lost his way and never found the cottage, following the wrong stream too far downhill. At last he purposely found his way back to the barn where he had slept the night before, crept through the cat-door, and shot into the heap of straw again. He curled up and pretended that he was back on the mountain top in the heart of the rock listening to thunder-winds outside. He went right to sleep.

13
SPYING AT BREAKFAST

HUNGER WAS THE ALARM that kept Gibbie from sleeping long in the morning. He peeped first, then climbed out of the straw and climbed the ladder to the loft where the cheese was kept. He gnawed where he had gnawed before and greatly enlarged the hole. That made him instantly thirsty, and he hurried to the cat-door. But from there he saw the farmer examining his ricks, speculating about their market price. Gibbie backed up and looked for a place to hide in case the farmer came in.

There was a ladder at the far end of the barn near a kind of cupboard door high in the wall. Gibbie scrambled up and stuck his head through the doorway too carelessly. He knocked a small dish off a shelf and it crashed on the stone floor of the next room. A woman rushed in crying, "Where is that bad cat!" Gibbie pulled his head back.

Seeing that the cat, which she couldn't find, had not got into any of her open containers of milk, she calmed down and picked up the broken dish and left. Gibbie had discovered the dairy room.

This room was oddly built, with a partial ceiling. By creeping along a high shelf Gibbie could get to the strong ceiling and safely peek down through the cracks between its boards. He saw the woman pour hot water from the pot into a large dish in which she washed other dishes;

he had never seen dishwashing before. He saw her clean the table and chairs. He saw a butter churn which he mistook for what an organ grinder played tunes on in city streets where he came from. He was shocked that the woman poured cream into the wooden organ and that when she turned the handle fast no music came out. He was shocked that she poured strange stuff out and that after she washed it and shaped it he recognized it as butter. Surely these people were well fed! All that butter!

Slowly Gibbie realized that country people are busy and careful and that things there belong to them. He began to perceive that just as shop owners must be paid for what they own, farmers might need to be paid also.

Gibbie watched the woman throw handful after handful of meal into the great boiling pot of water, stirring as she threw. Four men and one boy entered for breakfast. Gibbie felt starved as he watched them eat porridge and milk, and he saw what was left scooped into a dish. As soon as he could, he returned to the barn and crept out the cat-door. He knew now that he had done wrong to eat the cheese; it had belonged to someone. He was horribly ashamed.

But as he passed the chicken coop he spied the dish of leftover porridge inside. He had thought it would be saved for people to eat later. Gibbie felt fine about joining animals as they ate. He felt at home with them. He climbed in, scooped up some porridge while the hens pecked at it, and trotted away to the stream greatly refreshed.

14
FINDING DONAL GRANT

GIBBIE SET OUT ALONG THE STREAM to return to the river and continue up Daurside. He came to an open meadow of rye-grass and clover where cows were grazing. They were guarded by the very boy whom Gibbie had peeked down upon from his perch above the kitchen breakfast scene a bit earlier. Now the boy was reading a book and didn't see Gibbie approaching from behind.

A certain black cow with short sharp horns and a wicked look had been edging nearer the cornfield that lay beyond a low wall of mossy earth. Suddenly she ran for it, jumped the low wall, and began tearing and gobbling the corn. Like a shot Gibbie was after her to stop her. At that instant the cowherd sprang up, grabbed his big stick, and ran to save Gibbie as well as the corn. He knew that this malicious cow would gladly gore an unarmed child with her horns. She was so eager to fight that she was named Gore. The only reason she hadn't been sold to the butcher was that she was a splendid milker.

The boy kept shouting warnings to Gibbie, but Gibbie supposed the boy was yelling at the cow. He ran straight at Gore and tried to shove her toward the wall. She was so startled that she bolted. Then she saw her cowherd coming with the stick and turned back toward Gibbie. In contempt she lowered her head and charged at him. He hit her on her horn with a stone, and then the cowherd delivered a storm of blows with his big stick and she returned to the meadow in defeat. Drawing himself up with a swell of success, Donal Grant looked down on Gibbie with admiration.

"Hey, creature!" he said, "you're more of a man than you look at about age seven. What got into you to risk the devil's horns? If it hadn't been for my club we would both be over the moon by this time. What do they call you?"

Gibbie only smiled.

"Where do you come from? Where's your folks? Where do you stay?"

Gibbie burst out laughing, he was so delighted to hear someone talk to him. He liked this boy.

"The creature's stupid," Donal decided sadly. "Poor thing!" he said aloud as he laid his hand on Gibbie's head.

No human had touched Gibbie kindly for many weeks, and his unmingled delight burst out in a perfect smile.

"Come, creature, and I'll give you a snack. You can understand that," said Donal as he headed toward the meadow where Gore was eating with the other cows, looking meek and mild.

Gibbie followed Donal, who walked slowly because he was reading his book as he went along. Back in the middle of the meadow he looked up at last, a bit bewildered.

"I hope none of them swallowed my sack lunch," he mused. "I'm not sure where I was sitting. I have my place in my book, but I lost my place in the meadow."

Gibbie was already flitting back and forth and in another minute he pounced upon Donal's lost sack and brought it to him in triumph.

"You're not the moron I took you for," Donal said thoughtfully. He took out a piece of oatcake for Gibbie and leaned against the low wall to read. Gibbie sat cross-legged, ate his snack, and gazed at Donal. It seemed like paradise to be with him. Donal's face was burned brown by the sun and covered with freckles. His hair was reddish-brown, and his eyes were brownish-green. Donal was strongly built for a boy almost fifteen, with a friendly honest look about him. He was lost in his book for minutes at a time.

Gibbie could not imagine why anyone would be interested in a book, because all he knew of books was what he had seen that one miserable morning in the old woman's school. But he could imagine how bothersome it was for someone so interested in a book to be interrupted by cows that kept going into the cornfield. So as Donal watched his book, Gibbie watched the herd and silently took Donal's club. Before long Donal saw Gore in the corn again and Gibbie fighting her with the club.

"Give it to her on the nose," Donal shouted in terror as he rushed to help. Gibbie heard and obeyed and then Gore ran back to the meadow.

"You must come from fighting folk," Donal said with admiration.

Gibbie laughed with sweat pouring down his face. They returned to their places. Gibbie had found someone to help at last. A whole human being and about twenty-five animals besides! He admired Donal's suit of worn-out green corduroy with brass buttons on the jacket. Donal's short trousers had patches instead of holes at the knees, and below his trousers were warm woolen stockings and solid shoes. On his head Donal had a small blue cap. Inside his head Donal was thinking about Gibbie, who looked so neglected yet so special.

At lunch time Donal gave Gibbie one-third of his food, and Gibbie offered part back to Donal, and Donal refused with a smile. Gibbie was as happy as a prince would like to be. Awhile later, Donal looked up from his book and saw Gibbie fascinated by a single beautiful daisy. Donal forgot that he himself had loved daisies before he ever read how the poet Robert Burns described them, and foolishly thought that Gibbie must have been reading Robert Burns if he loved a daisy this much.

"Can you read, creature?" asked Donal.

Gibbie shook his head no.

"Can't you speak, fellow?"

Again Gibbie shook his head.

"Can you hear?"

Gibbie burst out laughing. He knew he heard better than other people.

"Listen to this then."

Donal took his book from the grass and read an old Danish ballad that was rewritten in English by Sir Walter Scott. Gibbie's eyes grew wider and wider as he heard the lilting words, and his mouth fell slightly open. When Donal finished, Gibbie stayed that way for a time; then he slid over and peeked into the book. It was like looking into a well for water and seeing only dry pebbles and sand inside. Gibbie saw nothing in the book at all like what he had heard.

Neither cold nor hunger nor rags nor loneliness had ever brought tears to Gibbie's eyes, but now Gibbie had tears of sorrow because the beautiful words were gone. Donal understood and asked Gibbie if he would like to hear it again. Gibbie's face answered with a flash, and Donal read the poem again for him. Then he read it a third time and closed the book. He had never seen such a look of thankfulness on anyone's face before.

For the rest of his life, whenever Gibbie thought about beautiful things made by humans, he always remembered that day in the meadow with Donal Grant when he first began to come awake to the human world of thoughts and feelings, loves and delights. Gibbie threw himself into the deep grass, more or less in a daze.

After Donal had gathered the cows he could not see Gibbie so he thought he had left for his family. Donal watered the cows and tied them in their stalls at last, ate supper, did his next geometry lesson, and went to bed.

15
TWO HUNGRY MINDS

HUNGRY MINDS ARE AS FREQUENT among peasant people as anywhere else. So it is not surprising that a Scottish cowherd like Donal happened to be eager to learn. Education was cheap in Scotland in those days, but Donal's parents were too poor to dream of sending a son to college. Donal's older brothers and sisters had helped his parents pay the small cost of his childhood education, which was not free in those days.

Now, Donal supported himself as a cowherd, and had a wonderful opportunity to learn. That was because of Fergus Duff. Fergus was Farmer Duff's second son, a college student who lived at home from the first of April to the end of October. Fergus was not very healthy and was a bit proud besides, so he did not help on his father's farm. He enjoyed Donal and entertained himself by lending books to Donal and teaching him things he had learned at college. Donal was a superb student.

Donal looked up to Fergus as one of the lords of the world. Neither young man realized that Fergus had far less talent than his father's herdboy, and Donal fed Fergus's pride with his great gratitude. Now, for the first time, Donal had the experience of feeling tender toward a grateful young learner when he met Gibbie.

Gibbie lay cold and hungry in the meadow, feeling warm and full.

He thought he was alone except for the wind and shadow, the sky and closed daisies. But there was a presence with him and in him that he did not know about. Later he would learn about life. Now he watched the stars come out like a herd grazing in blue pastures. He was very sleepy, so he trotted back to the barn and wormed his way through the cat-hole.

The straw was gone! But he remembered the hay. He groped his way through the dark loft and burrowed into the hay like a sand-fish in wet sand. As he slept, he heard the breath of the white horse in the next room. Early in the morning the horses awakened him.

16

THE SECRET HELPER

GIBBIE SCRAMBLED UP AND GAZED at the beautiful white horse. For the first time in his life he wondered if he was as clean as he should be. He decided to check on that at the stream later. He tried feeding the horse some hay, but it was still full of grass from the night before and wouldn't look at hay.

Gibbie wanted to watch the woman do kitchen work again, so he dragged the barn ladder into place and crept onto the shelf above the kitchen. It was empty, and it was a mess. He clambered down and began to do everything he had seen the woman do. He swept the floor, dusted the tables and chairs, and started the fire. Then he heard footsteps and darted into the dairy and climbed onto the kitchen ceiling to peek down through a large crack.

"I must have been walking in my sleep!" the woman exclaimed. Her name was Jean Mavor and she was Farmer Duff's half-sister. "Or that good boy Donal Grant's been helping me. He's good enough for any-thing—even to become a minister!"

Gibbie eagerly watched all she did and planned to do more the next morning. He wanted to watch the men eat breakfast, but his own hunger made him feel sick. He sneaked down to the stream to drink, then to the meadow to wait for Donal Grant. The first that Donal saw of Gibbie was Gibbie's attack with rocks upon Gore in the cornfield.

"You mustn't use stones," he said. "It's not right for me to find fault, though," he added, "reading books like a lout and letting the cows ruin the corn when I'm paid to keep them out of it. I'm disgusted with myself."

Gibbie answered by running to get the book and pressing it into Donal's hands, then circling the cows with Donal's club and forcing Gore far from the cornfield. Donal saw that Gibbie meant to do the work for him, and Gibbie did it perfectly. Donal read and read.

At lunchtime when Donal opened his sack lunch prepared by Jean Mavor he found far more good food than usual. He could guess from Gibbie's eyes that he was starving. "She must have guessed there were two of us," Donal exclaimed.

Little did Donal guess that Jean was rewarding him for helping her in the kitchen, and that Gibbie's eager hands had done the work for her. Rewards don't often come that directly even when good deeds are done openly.

Before the day was over Donal chose a time when the cows were behaving well and had Gibbie sit down to listen to another ballad. One couldn't tell who enjoyed the poem more—the reader or the listener.

After Donal took the cows home that evening Gibbie lay still, wondering how Donal got all those strange beautiful sounds and words out of the book.

17
MORE AND MORE HELP

EVERY MORNING GIBBIE GOT INTO the kitchen early enough to do more work and do it better, until all Jean had to do was make the porridge at the last minute. She thought Donal Grant was her helper and kept giving him extra large lunches in appreciation. At night she put out plenty of cloths and towels, and in the morning everything was ready when she came in. All the supper dishes were washed and put away, the water was boiling for porridge, and the butter was perfectly made. She wondered how a boy could learn to do her work so well.

Gibbie could have continued weeks longer as a secret kitchen worker if he had not also begun to do secret stable work. He groomed horses and polished brass and put hay in the racks. He did not know that the men who worked with the horses did not appreciate this because they were jealous and suspicious.

Meanwhile, as Gibbie cleaned the butter churn and so much else, he got the idea of cleaning himself also. Every evening he bathed in the Lorrie, the largest of the little streams that flowed down from Glashgar into the Daur river. He even learned to swim there. Grooming horses gave him the idea of washing and smoothing his thick shiny hair.

Every day Gibbie worked for Donal, and Donal fed him and read to him. When Donal asked about his family Gibbie looked sad, and when Donal asked where Gibbie slept, Gibbie laughed. But as Donal read to Gibbie it helped Donal to think more clearly about what he was reading, and so he learned more. Donal did not realize how close he felt to the little boy who could not speak. The cows became very fond of Gibbie also—all except Gore.

Even when some late sleet and rain came in June and Donal could not take books out into the meadow, Gibbie was there in his few tattered rags to laugh and help.

18
THE BROWNIE

THINGS HAD GONE ON THIS WAY for several weeks when one morning the men came to breakfast complaining loudly about their secret helper. Gibbie never heard what was said at breakfast. The men suspected Fergus Duff of doing the work because his favorite horse Snowball always got special treatment. Actually, they had less work to do now. But they feared that Fergus was preparing to find fault with them to his father somehow, and that one of them might lose his job.

Gibbie had found oats in a bin and had been feeding the horses too much of what was meant to be a treat for them. As a result, that day the overfed Snowball cheerfully dumped Fergus into a ditch and galloped home without him. When Fergus heard the workers say it served him right for interfering with their chores before breakfast, he exclaimed in a huff that he was busy studying before breakfast. The plain fact that he was sound asleep at that time of day would have been more truthful and more convincing.

That evening Jean warned Donal that he was carrying his good deeds too far and asked him why he wasted good oats on the horses. Donal was so bewildered that Jean realized that he was not her secret helper after all. For a moment she was almost angry at him, but her good sense came back to her. If Donal was not the helper, who was? Not Fergus. She knew her nephew Fergus too well to imagine that he would bother to help other people

As Donal apologized for not being her helper after all, Jean suddenly stared in silence with her deep-set gray eyes. Finally she said in a low, broken voice, "Donal, it's the brownies!"

Donal's mouth fell open. He had been taught in school that there are no elves, but long ago he had heard old folks talk about an elf-like creature called a brownie. It had haunted this farm when the old folks' grandparents were young. Donal shivered with horror and delight.

"Do you really think there are such creatures as brownies, Mistress Jean?"

"Who knows what there is and what there isn't?" she answered guardedly. "Hold your tongue about it. Least said is soonest mended. Get to your work." Not wanting to meet a brownie, Jean had a new habit of staying in bed two hours longer than she used to before her secret helper started doing her work. The less said the better.

That very night the rumor spread to nearby farms that the *Mains of Glashruach farm was haunted by a brownie. One morning Gibbie carefully braided Snowball's long thick mane into countless lovely strands. That added to the rumor. At last the mighty rumor came all the way to the owner of the House of Glashruach himself.

*In Scotland, farms that belong to a nearby mansion are sometimes called the mains of the mansion. British people often give their farms special names.

19
THE CRUEL LORD
OF GLASHRUACH

THOMAS GALBRAITH HAD A PECULIAR PAST. His name was Thomas Durrant, and he married the woman who inherited Glashruach. They decided to be called Mr. and Mrs. Galbraith instead of Mr. and Mrs. Durrant, using her famous last name instead of his plain one. She died fairly young and left him with her last name, custody of her property, and their daughter. He had never felt that the property was quite his own until his wife was out of the picture, and when she died he consoled himself rather easily by concentrating upon all he had gained through the marriage. She had been like a ladder to success for him, and he didn't miss the lost ladder much at all. He ignored the legal fact that the property should have passed on to his daughter because it had to pass to a Galbraith by birth—not by marriage.

The only fight that Mr. and Mrs. Galbraith ever had was over the name of their daughter. He wanted the girl named Thomasina after him and the mother insisted upon a popular name of that day—Ginevra. The mother won, but the father was so resentful that he always called the girl Ginny instead.

Mr. Galbraith had been an Edinburgh lawyer before his marriage. He was very tall and very thin, with a small head, a large soft-looking nose, a loose-lipped mouth, and very little chin. His brown hair looked like a wig and his pale blue eyes, too large for their sockets, never seemed in focus at the same time. He always looked as if he had to hold himself together, and rather resembled a long-necked hen very proud of her eggs. He had great respect for his respectability. He was no good at farming, and so he rented out his land to farmers and then interfered as much as possible. He almost always looked displeased, but he meant to look dignified instead.

The one thing that displeased Mr. Galbraith more than anything else was what is called "superstition." Although he believed all kinds of things that were not true at all, he hated any kind of superstition or fable with far more enthusiasm than he hated sin. He had no real interest in truth. But the mere mention of the word ghost would turn his face into an ugly sight to see. Nothing challenged him so much as his desire to stamp out stories about the supernatural. He was a dull man with few interests, and his dearest interest was his scorn for superstition.

Unfortunately, he took little interest in his daughter Ginevra, to whom he was very cold. He was never harsh to her, but most children would prefer to be kissed at times and spanked at times rather than neither. She was a solemn-looking little girl, almost nine years old, who dressed in very plain brown clothes and wore her brown hair in braids down her back tied with black ribbons. She looked uninteresting unless one saw the life and feeling that sometimes appeared in her eyes. Ginevra felt guilty that when she asked herself if she loved her father better than anyone else, as she believed she ought, she couldn't feel any love for him at all.

The fact is that a child can't feel very close to a father who dislikes childhood and purposely forgets he was a child. It is the fatherly feelings in a child and the childlike feelings in a father that reach to each other eternal hands and love. Ginevra couldn't even have touched her father with her real hands at meals if she had tried. He made her sit at the other end of the long dining table.

One day at lunch Ginevra dared to ask her father what a brownie is.

"What is the meaning of this, Joseph?"
Mr. Galbraith asked his butler in some anger.

"What foolish person has been insinuating such contemptible superstition into your silly head?" he demanded.

"They say there's a brownie at the Mains who does all the work."

"What is the meaning of this, Joseph?" Mr. Galbraith asked his butler in some anger.

"The meaning of what, sir?" returned Joseph coolly. (He used to say of his unpleasant employer in private, "He's not really a Galbraith.")

The lord gave a speech about his horror that hired servants would spread superstition in his own house, using their tongues as if they had no more sense than a bunch of bells ringing, teaching his daughter folly. He got Joseph to tell him the rumor that invisible hands were doing the farm work at night at the Mains. Hearing that, he clenched his teeth in anger and for a whole moment said nothing.

"I shall soon be at the bottom of it," he said at last. "Go to the Mains at once, Joseph, and ask Fergus Duff to come here as soon as he can."

Fergus was pleased to visit the lord and although he had taken little interest in the matter until now he was happy to help the lord investigate.

"Then Fergus, since kitchen utensils can't fly, all you have to do is to watch and see who moves them. The answer will be simplicity itself."

Fergus headed home a bit unhappy. He would sit up all night, if necessary, to catch the culprit. He didn't believe in brownies. He was almost eighteen. He couldn't admit to himself that he was frightened of brownies at night whether they exist or not.

20

AN ANGRY AMBUSH

WHEN THE HOUSE WAS QUIET THAT NIGHT Fergus crept to the kitchen and read stories in an old book by candlelight. Once he dozed and awakened in a fright. After he had finished the book, terrors really tortured him for hours. If an animal outside had made a noise Fergus would have shamed himself by shrieking and awakening the sleepers for nothing. He believed in no night invaders but ordinary robbers, yet he was afraid to look behind him for fear a brownie was there. When at last the cock crowed for morning, Fergus jumped up in fear that became relief. He lay down on the kitchen bench to rest his back, laughing at his night fears. He was asleep in a moment. Gibbie crept in, saw him, and crept out. Just then Fergus awoke, stretched, and went away to bed. In came the brownie and did all the work.

Fergus was hours late for breakfast and found his auntie Jean there alone.

"Well, auntie," he boasted, "I think I got rid of your brownie!"

"Did you?" she exclaimed. "And then did all the work yourself to help me?"

"No, no. I was too tired for that. I had sat up all night."

"Who did it then?"

"You must have done it yourself, auntie."

"If you chased away one brownie, another came, Fergus. I didn't lift a finger. The work's done, same as ever."

"A curse on the creature!" cried Fergus.

"Shush that! He may be listening. I don't like swearing."

"I'm sorry, auntie, but it's provoking." He told her his night story but left out the fact he had been scared. After breakfast he went to Glashruach.

The lord was displeased and told him to sleep in advance and watch better. The next night he was as terrified as before but stayed awake until his aunt arrived. He had caught no brownie, but her kitchen was a complete mess as she had left it in the evening. Jean could see no good in this change at all and gave Fergus little thanks. He crawled off to bed rather mortified. When he got up much later she had fixed him no meal, so he had to fix himself a snack and set out to report to the lord.

"You must add cunning to courage, my young friend!" Mr. Galbraith advised, and sent him home. Fergus went to bed for the afternoon.

There was a tiny pantry in the kitchen with room for just one chair in it. Fergus squeezed himself and a chair in with the door wide open. He obeyed the lord's orders and lit no candle. As a result he went right to sleep accidentally and slept all night on the chair.

He awakened at the first sound Gibbie made. It was broad daylight but Fergus was frightened. He peeped out. There in the place of a big ugly brownie he saw a tiny boy in rags with beautiful hair and blue eyes, quick hands and silent bare feet, doing all the work. Gradually he became deeply angry that all his fear and inconvenience had been caused by a mere child. Gibbie heard Fergus's chair creak and darted away through the dairy into the barn. Fergus went around to corner him in the barn. Gibbie escaped through the cat-door, but Fergus simply unlocked the door and chased him down to the stream. Gibbie was a better runner, but Fergus's legs were almost twice as long. Up the mountainside they ran.

Just at the iron gate to Glashruach Fergus grabbed Gibbie. Gibbie's happy smile of defeat would have softened a harder heart than Fergus's, but Fergus had lost his temper entirely about the whole matter. Gibbie's smile was answered by a blow on the side of his head. As he looked pitifully at Fergus with his smile fading, Fergus hit him just as hard on the other side. The balance of the blows was hardly any help, and Gibbie's ears rang and his eyes watered and his head ached. Fergus started asking Gibbie questions, and when Gibbie said no words, Fergus banged him again on both sides of his head, boxing his ears. Disgusted at taking such a pitiful child to the lord after their big plans, Fergus threatened Gibbie with prison and ripped the collar half off his old jacket. Then he marched him to the big house, shaking him so hard at times that it made Gibbie's teeth ache.

So Sir Gibbie Galbraith approached the rich country house of his ancestors for the first time. He had no idea at all that history had cheated him of this very inheritance. It would have made little difference to him if he had known all the past stories of his family; he would still have accepted whatever came to him as part of his own present story. He did not know it, but in a sense his story had barely begun. It was going to move much faster now.

21

NEAR MURDER

GIBBIE'S ONLY EXPERIENCE WITH THE LAW until now had been with the city police, who liked him, and he had no fear of authorities. He approached the great old stone house with no fear of punishment, knowing he had done no wrong.

Mr. Galbraith always awakened early, and so he considered early rising a virtue no matter how one spent the morning after getting up. This morning was one in which Mr. Galbraith would have been far more virtuous in bed asleep. He was talking to Angus, who oversaw his animals, by the coach-house door when Fergus appeared with Gibbie. A more innocent-looking captive never appeared before a lawyer. But Mr. Galbraith judged people largely by their clothes, and so Gibbie's rags made him look like a hardened criminal in Mr. Galbraith's peculiar eyes. He smiled a grim, ugly smile.

"So this is your famous brownie, Mr. Duff!" he said with contempt.

"It's all the brownie I could lay hands on, sir," answered Fergus. "I caught him in the act."

"Boy, what have you to say for yourself?" The lord's eyes rolled worse than usual in his excitement.

If Gibbie could have spoken the truth he would have been called a liar anyway, but all he could do was smile.

"What is your name?"

Gibbie smiled trustingly. He had no idea that grown men who were not drunk could be cruel. He thought the questions were only to tease him; he did not guess that he was really expected to answer.

"Here, Angus," the lord said calmly. "Take him into the coach-house and teach him a little behavior. The whip will loosen his tongue."

Angus led Gibbie inside and stripped him naked, glad to punish him for being a tramp and a thief. He approached with the heavy cart whip and saw Gibbie lift his brown arms in silent appeal beside his thin white body. In fact Gibbie had no idea of what the whip could do to him.

Assuming he was to be beaten for the few bites of cheese he had eaten weeks before, Gibbie bowed his head. At the last minute Angus put down the heavy whip and used a lighter whip instead. Otherwise he would almost surely have killed Gibbie with the first blow. Gibbie was faint with hunger as well as being a very small boy.

The first blow looked as if the lash had cut Gibbie in two at the waist. A huge red welt bled across his back. The moment the whip struck him Gibbie shivered all over and dropped soundlessly to the ground. In fact his heart briefly stopped beating.

"Up with you, devil!" Angus raged as he lifted the whip again and lashed. This stroke ran all the way down the center of Gibbie's back from his neck to the end of his spine. Angus's arm was up for the third blow when a piercing shriek made him pause.

In ran Ginevra, out of her head with horror. She stood over Gibbie's body and shook and screamed as if she were a woman torn out of heaven and cast into hell.

"Go away, miss," cried Angus. "He's a bad creature who must be whipped."

Ginevra lifted one of Gibbie's hands to try to raise him, and his arm hung limp and motionless. When she let it go it dropped like a stick and she began to shriek again. When Angus saw Gibbie's white face he felt a tinge of fear himself. Child-murder could cause some trouble.

"He's died! He's died! You've killed him, Angus!" she cried fiercely. "I hate you. I'll tell on you: I'll tell my papa."

"Shush, miss," said Angus. "It is by your father's own orders I am whipping him and he well deserved it. If you don't go away and be a good young lady, I'll go on whipping him."

"I'll tell God," Ginevra screamed, and clung to Gibbie so that Angus couldn't get her away.

"If you dare to touch him again, Angus, I'll bite you—*bite you*—BITE YOU!" she screamed with incredible force for a small girl.

The lord and Fergus had walked away a bit as if feeling guilty about the beating; when they heard the wild cries they assumed it all came from Gibbie rather than Ginevra. Other members of the household tried to rush in to investigate, but the lord ordered them all back to work.

Ginevra's shrieks roused Gibbie. In his confusion he thought his pain was hers and reached his hand to her tear-stained face to comfort her. In a fury Angus caught Ginevra up and carried her away; she was clawing and biting him like a cat. He never admitted to anyone that she bit his arm so hard it left a scar.

The moment they disappeared Gibbie began to understand that she was grieving for his pain, not he for hers. This was like the place where men had murdered Sambo. This was evil. Would they hurt the little girl? He felt sure she was safe; she was at home. After several tries he got to his feet. He was struggling to put his rags back on when he thought he heard a step. He dropped the rag and fled naked into the wind.

When the three men discovered that their victim had escaped and left his two rags behind they were disgusted at such lack of modesty. They thought he was a stupid naked savage. Other eyes would have seen him as an angel.

In his hunger and pain Gibbie ran in aimless terror, feeling that the three men were right behind him. At last he had crossed a stream and come to a large hill where he felt safer. He got the idea that Angus was the very person with a gun whom Donal Grant had once pointed out to him far away. Donal said the man had shot and killed a man who had entered the lord's property to steal some food. Perhaps Gibbie would get shot now and lie still and be put into a hole in the earth and covered up. This idea drove him farther and farther, hiding always under heather and behind bushes.

Gibbie now owned three physical possessions that could be separated from his body—his hair, his nails, and his huge hunger. In his mind he had what he could recall of a ballad about a fair lady that Donal had taught him. And in his suffering body he had splendid health, in his heart great courage, and in his soul an ever-throbbing love. It was that love of humans that caused his horror of Angus; Angus was human but was not human. An "unman."

Poor Ginevra was sent to bed for misbehavior and after her rage and horror and pity a great hopelessness possessed her. Her dutiful affection for her father was greatly weakened for the rest of her life.

Fergus told his aunt the story as if it were quite a joke. But the more Jean thought about the affair, the less she liked it. What had they whipped the creature for? What harm had he done? He had taken nothing! Not a spoonful of food was ever missing. Her nephew had not solved the mystery at all; he had only sealed it up and spoiled it. She liked to think that the brownie had enchanted all three men into seeing him as a little boy and had really escaped unharmed. Indeed, the country people thought the lord's explanation of their brownie was far too unreasonable and incomplete to make good sense, and so if anything he increased their belief in brownies by clumsily trying to change their minds.

Donal Grant heard enough when he came home from his first day in the meadow without Gibbie to realize what an incredible child had been his friend and helper. Now Donal began to realize how much more he had been learning from books while Gibbie was there. Donal did not yet realize how Gibbie had been planting seeds of special gentleness, trust, loving service and absolute unselfishness in Donal's mind. Donal had also done much more for Gibbie than he knew.

What Donal thought he had been giving Gibbie, half the large and delicious sack lunches from Jean, was in truth much more a gift from Gibbie to Donal. Gibbie had earned all that special food that Jean gave to Donal, a fact neither of them understood as they had shared it those happy days in the meadow.

22

GIBBIE'S HIDING PLACE

IT WAS A LOVELY SATURDAY EVENING on Glashgar. The heather was not in bloom yet and there were no trees near the cottage where Janet and Robert Grant lived, but a noisy stream flowed beside their little field of oats and potatoes and the tiny cabbage garden bordered by daisies, primroses, and carnations. Janet tended the garden and Robert grew the oats and potatoes, and cared for a few sheep for the farmer at the Mains, who let the old couple live in the cottage. They had extremely little money, no debt, no fear, much love, and Janet's joy in her idea of the next life. They both suffered from rheumatism, but Janet said that was to teach them patience because they had no other trouble.

Robert often knelt and prayed out in the beauty of the mountainside with only his dog Oscar watching. Robert kept growing wiser and better without knowing it. He thought he had a dull soul, but he believed that his beloved Janet was especially close to the Father of Lights.

Janet had been cleaning the rafters of her cottage that afternoon with a broom on the end of a long stick. Cobwebs and soot were up there. In such a humble cottage people didn't bother to clean their rafters in those days. But that morning at breakfast a clap of thunder had made the cottage tremble and a piece of soot had dropped into Robert's spoon as he lifted it to his mouth. Janet decided that it wasn't decent to leave soot on the rafters any longer, and she wanted to do the job just as soon as possible just in case Jesus returned soon.

"Who knows when Jesus may be at the door?" Janet said to herself. "I wouldn't want him to say, 'Janet, you could have done your house a bit cleaner when you knew I might be coming!' "

When she finished at last she took her broom out to beat it clean against a rock, then stood looking along the path down the hill. Every Saturday evening her grown children came up the path one by one from their various jobs in the valley. All week Janet and Robert's thoughts constantly hovered around their children in the valley as if to watch them and ward off evil. Every Saturday they had a reunion.

Now as Janet looked into the light of the sinking sun she thought she saw the body of a child staggering up the path, hands groping. She covered her eyes and looked again. She thought she saw naked white skin with sun-red streaks on it. It was the same child who had visited her so strangely before! He held out his hands and fell at her feet face-down. In horror Janet saw the great cross-shaped wound on his bare back.

For one instant she stood half-stunned as she looked at the motionless child and thoughts of Jesus still suffering and delivering us moved vaguely in her mind. Jesus is the one rock where evil finds no echo. Jesus is the cavern of destroying love into which all evil tumbles and finds no reaction and ends forever. All that and more in the first instant, and in the second instant she lifted him and carried him tenderly into the house murmuring dovelike sounds. She laid him on his side in her bed, covered him tenderly, and hurried to get him some warm milk.

When she returned he had wearily opened his eyes. She set down the milk and went to him. Gibbie put up his arms, threw them around her neck, and clung to her as if she had been his mother. And from that moment on she was his mother. She kissed him.

"What have they done to you, my baby?" she said in pity.

No reply came except a smile of absolute content. What were wounds and nakedness and hunger to Gibbie, now that he had a woman to love! Gibbie absolutely had to give love; but here was more. Here was love in return. Except in Sambo he had rarely seen love before.

Janet raised him with one arm, held the bowl to his mouth, and he drank; but all the time his eyes were fixed on hers. When she laid him down again he was fast asleep in a moment. He lay so still she feared he was dead, but she felt his heart and it was beating steadily. With a glad heart she made him a bowl of her special porridge fit for a queen and set it near the fire for him. She was doing this for Jesus in the person of one of his little ones. Then she set the table for her grown sons and daughters.

As each of her children arrived Janet turned down the covers and showed the raw little back of her seventh child. The two daughters wept and the three sons were furious, each in his own way.

"Curse the rascal that did it!" one son cried in rage.

"Take that back," said Janet. "If you don't forgive your enemies, you'll not be forgiven yourself."

"That's a bit hard, Mother," he answered.

"Hard!" she echoed. "It may be hard, all right. But what would be the use of God forgiving you or how could you appreciate it if you are carrying a hell of hate in your own heart? My son, those who won't forgive their enemies carry a nest of evil inside."

"Well, he's not *my* enemy," her son answered.

"Not your enemy!" returned Janet. "Not your enemy after treating a child like that? He's the enemy of all mankind. He has *me* for an enemy, for sure, and as my enemy I forgive him. I hope he will really grieve over this sin some day."

"Now, now, Mother," said another son. "That sounds as bad as what Jock said."

"What? Would you have the man enter eternity without grieving over such a wicked sin? What good would that do him? I wish him the

78

best I can when I wish him painful shame and sorrow. I'll probably be dead before he asks God's forgiveness, because it takes time for such a mean person to come to his holy senses."

Just then the sixth of Janet's children entered and she led him to the bed.

"The Lord preserve us!" cried Donal Grant. "It's my friend." He began to choke. "He's been with me every day for weeks until today."

Donal told about the brownie, and Janet warned him to keep the boy's location secret. Donal saw the sense in that, but decided that if Fergus was guilty he would never speak to him again.

Gibbie's blue eyes opened and looked at Donal, who darted to him and took Gibbie's face between his hands. Gibbie smiled.

"Do you think the beating took away his speech?" Janet asked.

"No, no," answered Donal. "He's been like that since I met him. I never heard a word from his mouth."

"He must be deaf and dumb," said Janet.

"He's not deaf, Mother. That I know well. But he must be dumb. If you hear me, boy, pinch my nose."

With a laugh Gibbie pinched Donal's big nose, and everyone broke out laughing. It was as if they had found an angel's baby in the bushes and had been afraid he was an idiot and were all relieved. Janet brought him his porridge and although he moaned with pain while sitting up, Gibbie smiled at them all with absolute bliss as he took the bowl. His look at Janet showed that he had never tasted anything so delicious before.

Janet brought out a plain white gown of hers and put it on Gibbie. It was cool and soft on his sore skin. Just then Robert got home and had to hear the entire story. When Gibbie heard the part about the brownie for the first time, he broke into laughter and they all laughed. But Robert never said a word. Except for sometimes with his wife, the old man said almost as little as Gibbie about his deep feelings.

The family sat down to a supper of porridge that no one but Janet could make, oatcakes that only she could bake, and milk that only Crummie her cow could give. Gibbie sat watching like a king on his throne. This was his own kingdom, because love is the best kind of ownership. Whenever someone looked his way his face lit up with love and merry gratitude.

After supper Janet had her children make Gibbie a little bed next to hers. They knew how to do it quickly. They gathered lots of heather bushes from outside and packed them together inside a simple frame made of boards, as if the heather were growing evenly and tightly from the floor toward the rafters. They spread a blanket over the heather and then a large linen sheet which lay under Gibbie and folded over him, and then a blanket on top. Gibbie sank into the soft bed with a sigh.

Donal placed the big Bible before his father and lit the wick of a little iron lamp, and Robert put on his reading glasses and found his place. He always did this before his children left. He was not a very good reader and often lost his place, but when that happened he simply filled in with his words as if he were telling Bible stories as he used to do when the children were little. He told the story of Christ healing the leper.

Then Robert led the family in prayer, depending upon phrases he had learned long ago although he did not understand exactly what the words meant. What mattered was that he was lifting his heart up to God. Gibbie had no idea what the prayer meant, but it lulled him to sleep. When he awakened later because of his pain the cottage was dark and the old couple were asleep.

Gibbie found something large and hairy lying next to him. It was a dog. He fell fast asleep again, if possible happier than ever.

23
GIBBIE'S TEACHER

As soon as Donal had the chance he asked Fergus what part he had played in Gibbie's beating. Fergus rudely asked what business a mere cowherd had to question him about his actions.

"It's this way, you see, Fergus: you have been uncommon good to me and I'm more obliged than I can say. But I would be a scoundrel to borrow books from you and avoid asking you what happened and suspect in my heart that you had been cruel and wrong. What was the child punished for? Tell me that. According to your aunt's own account he had taken nothing and had done nothing but good."

"Why didn't he speak up then and defend himself instead of being so damned stubborn?" returned Fergus. "He wouldn't tell his name or even where he came from. It was by the lord's orders that Angus MacPholp whipped him. I had nothing to do with it." Fergus left out the fact that he had hit Gibbie hard on both sides of the head first.

"Fergus! The boy is as silent as a worm. I don't believe he ever spoke a word in his life."

This news cut Fergus to the heart, for he was not without decency and pity. Unfortunately, Fergus wanted to feel all right instead of doing right. He was too proud to confess to Donal that he had done wrong. Donal was far, far below Fergus socially. And the little rascal who couldn't talk was nothing but a tramp. If he didn't deserve punishment this time, he had deserved it before and would deserve it again, so what was the fuss about?

Fergus went back to college with a cold spot in his heart where his friendliness to Donal had been. This time he didn't provide any of his books for Donal to study because he wanted Donal to be sad about losing him as a helpful friend. But Donal managed to borrow a book of the life and poetry of Robert Burns from someone else and couldn't have found a better book to study. He was sorry about Fergus, but he was thrilled with learning about Robert Burns.

In the meantime another relationship had died. Ginevra was not the same girl after Gibbie's beating as she was before. She had never managed to really love her father or feel comfortable with him, but now she was actually afraid of him. It showed in her face sometimes, but he never noticed. When she was very quiet because she was struggling with her fear of him, he figured she was sulking and ignored her as usual.

The morning after Gibbie arrived, he awakened with Janet's face beaming over him. She was going out to milk the cow and was concerned that he might awaken and run away. But when she saw the light in his eyes she knew he could not love her like that and leave her. She gave him porridge and milk and went out to her cow.

When she came back she found that Gibbie had swept the floor and washed the dishes and was examining an old shoe of Robert's to see if he could mend it. In return, Janet did some sewing she had been planning. She took a plain blue dress of hers and split the skirt and turned it into trousers so that Gibbie had something like a sailor suit to wear. It had no pockets, but Gibbie didn't mind that.

Then Janet sat and read in her New Testament and Gibbie watched with delight. He thought she was reading ballads like those Donal had read in the cow pasture. But Gibbie bothered Janet because she worshiped while she read, and she was used to doing this alone or with other worshipers.

82

"Can you read, little boy?"

Gibbie shook his head.

"Sit down then, and I'll read to you."

It was one of those love-awful, glory-sad chapters in the end of the Gospel of John, the darkest cloud of human sorrow shot through with eternal light. The name of Jesus may have reminded Gibbie of the last words of poor Sambo. Gibbie didn't understand the story, but tears rolled down his face for some reason.

Then Janet read Gibbie the parable of the prodigal son. He did not understand all the words, but caught the drift of the story. It reminded him of his own father whose home he used to return to every night. This poor example from real life made the story real to Gibbie because love is the key. At the end of the story Gibbie clapped his hands, shivered, and stood on one leg like a stork in his excitement. He laughed with joy.

Janet was satisfied because she understood his gladness, although many adults would have misunderstood and punished Gibbie for laughing. His laughter showed his joy in the reunion between the loving father and the sorry son.

Thus Gibbie had his first lesson in the most important subject there is. Janet never suspected how ignorant Gibbie was about Christianity. She thought that he must know as well as she the story of Jesus and the purpose of his life and death, and so she never tried to explain it. She just kept reading to Gibbie about Jesus, talking to him about Jesus, dreaming to him about Jesus until as the days went by somehow Gibbie's soul became full of the man, his doings, his words, his thoughts, his life. Jesus Christ was in him. Gibbie began to live for Jesus. Gibbie slept and waked and slept again—with the loveliest days between, at the cottage on Glashgar.

24
GIBBIE'S FIRST WORDS

FROM GIBBIE'S FIRST DAY AT THE COTTAGE he was as helpful to Janet as any of her daughters had ever been. But she insisted that Robert should take Gibbie out to help him in the hills also.

"He can't speak to the dog," Robert objected.

"The dog can't speak wither," retorted Janet, "but he understands. Who knows that he won't understand someone speechless like himself? You just try Gibbie. Tell him to tell the dog such and such and see what happens."

Robert made the experiment and it worked. Oscar obeyed Gibbie's gestures.

"The two creatures understand each other better than I understand either of them!" Robert told Janet.

Now it was the full glow of summer; the sweet keen air of the mountain bathed Gibbie as he ran and filled him with life. He and Oscar the collie were shepherds together helping old Robert, obeying his wishes with joy. Robert said he loved Gibbie as the very apple of his eye.

Gibbie was a city boy, but now he loved earth and sky, and soon knew the patterns of nature better than Robert himself. Often while Robert and Janet slept, Gibbie sat on a stone outside and watched the night sky. Gibbie never thought about himself, and so he was wide open to the joy of God's presence.

Every Saturday the brothers and sisters gathered, and dearest of all was Donal. Gibbie would have liked to go down and visit Donal at the farm, but Janet would not let him risk it so soon.

"Oh, but I wish I could find out about his family or where he came from or what they called him," she said. "Never one word."

"You should teach him to read, Mother."

"How do I do that, Donal? I would have to teach him to speak first."

But Donal had set her a challenge, and one day she got the idea of using writing instead of talking.

She went over the alphabet with Gibbie several times and had him make a large A on her slate with chalk. He already knew half the letters.

"*He's* no fool!" she said in triumph.

As soon as he knew the alphabet, she got her New Testament and told him what a word was, pointing out its letters, then asked him to write it on the slate from memory. Janet was not fussy about exact spelling, and Gibbie learned fast. When he began pondering over the book himself, asking Janet for help on new words, she knew he was understanding it and her heart leaped with joy.

One day she showed him the rhymed verses printed at the back of her Scottish Bible. He was so happy to read rhymed verses that he jumped up and laughed and danced and balanced on one leg.

A few weeks after this Janet noticed one day that Gibbie was working very hard on his slate. He had written *give* and *giving* at the top, and then *gib* and *gibing*. Then he wrote *giby* and jumped up with a radiant smile and handed the slate to Janet. Janet said, *"Jiby?"* He shook his head and pointed to the *g* in *give*. Then Janet said *"Giby?"* and he danced a moment. Then he worked longer. He wrote out from the Bible *Galatians* and *breath*, and under them *galbreath*.

Janet knew that the landlord's name was Thomas Galbraith, and so she wouldn't believe that Galbraith was this boy's name also. But he finally convinced her that he used to be called *Sir Giby Galbreath*. Sir Gibbie Galbraith! She questioned him until she found out that his father had called him that and that his father had repaired shoes.

From that moment on all the family called the boy Gibbie. But Galbraith was never mentioned—too dangerous, or too valuable, for a child in that part of the country.

25

RUMORS

GIBBIE WAS GROWING FAST AND GAINING strength and speed. One afternoon Donal was looking for him on the mountainside and came to a deep dark pool called "Dead Pot," which was frightening to look at. Something catapulted down and a loud splash echoed up the stones. Next Donal saw Gibbie and Oscar on the other side. Gibbie scrambled down where Oscar didn't dare to go. Twenty feet above the water Gibbie could climb no farther, so he dived into the only safe spot in the small lake. He pulled a baby lamb out of the icy water and ran up the hill to return it to its mother. That is when Donal realized what a good athlete Gibbie was.

The next summer Gibbie often practiced swimming at night in the Daur river. He also tamed all the goats on the mountainside, so that they didn't butt him and bruise him any more.

Every time Donal came home he brought ballads or songs or verse to read to Gibbie. Instead of growing used to poetry, Gibbie enjoyed it more and more. What Donal never guessed was that no matter what story Gibbie heard, he always asked himself what Jesus or a disciple of Jesus would do in that situation. There was much Gibbie did not understand about life, but he saw that the more he did right the more he would understand right. He lived so kindly and obediently that the reality of Christ grew upon him and Jesus seemed very close.

When the frost and snow arrived, Gibbie did more of Robert's work for him. One sheep died, and Robert got permission to keep the skin, which he and Janet made into a woolly leather garment for Gibbie.

Down in the valleys people claimed that the mountain was haunted by a wild boy dressed in hairy skin, a boy who could talk with animals but not with humans. Finally the mere mention of "the beast-idiot of Glashgar" was enough to send children running like scared rabbits into their houses. When Thomas Galbraith heard about this superstition he was furious and scolded Angus because he found that Angus's own children believed the rumor. It never occurred to either angry man that a boy might be living up the mountain and that it might be the very boy they had almost killed. Neither man was very smart.

When Robert learned from Janet and Donal about how smart Gibbie was in many ways, he asked Janet about sending Gibbie to school. Janet thought it over for three days.

"Yes, Robert," she finally answered, "there's lots to learn that would help me be a better Christian. It would be a sin not to let the boy learn. But who would bother to teach him?"

"Let him go down and learn all Donal can teach him first," Robert suggested. "He can learn from Donal some days and herd sheep for me some days and help you here on other days."

Gibbie was delighted and nodded his head when Robert warned him never to get caught again and never to tell anyone any more of his name than just "Gibbie." As Janet said, the boy's nod was worth as much as the best man's promise out loud.

Soon Donal was teaching Gibbie arithmetic, geometry, Scottish history, and even *Paradise Lost*, which they both enjoyed although they didn't understand much of it.

26

ANGUS'S LONG DAY

When Gibbie's second winter on the mountain came, he dressed warmly in his sheepskin coat and leggings made out of deer hide. Various valley children again claimed to have seen the beast-idiot running over big rocks like a goat. One day a son of Angus came home terrified, saying the beast had chased him. He didn't admit that he had been throwing stones at the sheep up the mountain and had been chased away from the sheep.

So one fine December morning Angus shouldered his double-barreled gun and set out in bright sun and cold wind to catch the savage. About noon he discovered Gibbie tending some sheep and trying to play a melody on a kind of whistle he had made. Angus saw the deer-skin on his legs and went into an idiotic rage, thinking that Gibbie had stolen one of Thomas Galbraith's deer. In fact, Donal had bought the pieces of deer hide in the village for Gibbie.

Gibbie saw Angus and started running. Angus took aim and shouted, then fired. He meant to fire buckshot, but he pulled the wrong trigger and a bullet went through Gibbie's leg.

Fortunately, the bullet passed between two muscles and didn't hit an artery. Gibbie jumped up from where he had fallen and kept on running. Oscar was terrified and ran with him. Angus chased them as fast as he could.

Janet was just taking the potatoes off the fire for dinner when the door flew open and Gibbie stumbled in and fell on the floor, bleeding. Robert heard Angus coming fast. He grabbed a huge rusty old broad-sword that wouldn't come out of its sheath because of the rust. He raised it over his head, eyes flashing, and brought it down on Angus as soon as he burst into their home. Angus staggered against the wall, and Robert socked him with his fist, knocking him to the floor. Oscar kept Angus there while Robert grabbed the gun.

"It's loaded," Angus warned.

"Then lie still," said Robert, pointing it at his head. "Your hour has come. This isn't the first person you have shot. I'm going to see if the sheriff can be persuaded to hang you. Quiet, or I'll save him the trouble!"

Then Robert had Janet hold the potato pot over Angus's head while Robert stepped outside to empty the shot out of the gun and lean it against the house. Whether Janet would have poured boiling water on Angus or not will never be known because Angus didn't dare move.

Gibbie finally revived enough to crawl to his bed, and Janet washed and bandaged his leg. Robert was guarding Angus.

"I'm going, Janet," Robert announced. "Run and get me your clothesline rope and we'll tie his hands and feet." Angus began to swear furiously, but Robert stood with his club ready and Janet tied Angus's feet. Then Angus cursed and struck at them as they began to tie his hands; but Robert warned him to lie still or get a sample of Oscar's teeth, and Angus gave in.

"I can't eat anything now. I'll take a biscuit along. Give Angus my dinner to fatten him for the gallows." So Robert left to get a public magistrate about five miles away, expecting to get home in about three hours.

Janet wanted to feed Angus, but he called her the worst names he knew. She sat down to eat her own meal, but his foul language made her nervous. He was in a rage because he was embarrassed as well as frightened, taken captive by an old man, a woman, and a collie. Hatred flowed from his mouth.

90

Then Robert had Janet hold the potato pot over Angus's head while Robert stepped outside to empty the shot out of the gun.

Janet stepped outside, fetched a jug of cold water, and from behind him poured it over Angus's face. He assumed that the water was boiling and let out a horrid yell. Janet knelt and wiped his face with her apron, warning him that she would pour water on him again any time he used bad language. He started to swear at her again, but managed to hold the words inside.

Soon Janet noticed that Angus must be planning to try to burn the cords around his wrists. She hurried out for a chain they sometimes used for cows and fastened it around his neck.

"Are you going to hang me, you she-devil?"

"You seem to want another drop of cold water," Janet answered. She fastened the chain to a stake in the clay floor and then stretched a rope from his hands to the door bolt and from his feet to a chest upon which she piled some stones. Now she thought she was safe enough and read in her Bible.

After an hour of silence Angus was more afraid. He knew that he was hated by everyone and that this would work against him if he had a trial. He began to beg Janet to let him go, claiming that his wife would start to worry about him. He even drank a little milk Janet offered him, hoping to soften her heart.

"No," she said, "you must just make the best of it. It's a good lesson in patience for you, one that you need. Robert will be back soon." With that, she went out to milk her cow.

In a little while, Gibbie tried to walk but had to crawl on his hands and knees, following Janet. Angus got a good look at his pale face and knew it was the little boy he had almost killed once before. He was twice as terrified as he had been, expecting Gibbie to murder him.

Actually, Gibbie had heard Janet's voice from outside and knew she was praying. He had often listened to her pray, and he was crawling out to hear what she was saying to her Master. She was kneeling down near the cow and praying to God for Angus. She knew he was dangerous but she still felt sorry for him and didn't want him to be hanged for shooting people. As Gibbie listened he figured out what had happened while he was unconscious. Gibbie decided to free the prisoner.

Angus pretended to be asleep when Gibbie came in. Gibbie looked for Janet's knife in vain and examined the huge knots. Then Gibbie put the tongs into the fire until the ends were red-hot. White-hot! Angus fully expected Gibbie to torture him and let out one terrific yell after another. Gibbie didn't know that Janet had wandered down the path and couldn't hear the racket just then; and so he bolted the door to keep her out while he freed the prisoner for her. Angus heard the bolt and was convinced that the beast-idiot was going to kill him. He screamed and struggled.

Angus made it hard for Gibbie to free him until he slowly realized that Gibbie was setting him loose by burning the cords. To Angus, Gibbie was a worthless idiot and he had an urge to belt him, but Gibbie held the hot tongs and Angus's hands were still tied. By the time Gibbie had struggled with the rope successfully and Angus was finally free to leave, he had seen enough of Gibbie's face up close to feel less like slapping him. He merely nodded in thanks, grabbed his gun, and rushed down the hill.

When Janet came in from milking she was astonished that Angus was gone. Gibbie's signs satisfied her. Robert returned late and alone. He was relieved that Angus was gone after all since the sheriff had been away.

The next day, Robert visited Angus to tell him that Gibbie didn't want to report Angus for shooting him. Angus was still angry but had enough sense to be courteous, saying his head would be sore for weeks.

Gibbie was the one who needed weeks for healing, but staying home with Janet was never a waste of time.

27
A VOICE

GIBBIE WAS A NURSE AS WELL AS A SHEPHERD that winter because Janet and Robert suffered much rheumatism during the rain and frost. After spending much of his childhood caring for drunkards and helping them home through midnight streets, caring for Robert and Janet was an honor; but Gibbie never compared people that way. One of his jobs was to put more peat on the fire during the night to keep the room warm, and that is why he was awake and overheard Robert and Janet in the middle of the night.

"I'm growing terrible old, Janet, and I can't feel happy about it. You see, I'm not used to it."

"That's true, Robert. If we had been born old we might be getting used to it by now."

"When I find myself so kind of helpless, I have it in my head that the Lord has forsaken me," Robert admitted.

"I wouldn't allow such a thought, Robert, so long as I knew I couldn't breathe or speak without him, for in him we live and move and have our being. If he's my life, why should I trouble myself about that life?"

"Yes, gal. But if you had this asthma making your chest as if it were lined with sandpaper that they had been lighting one or two thousand matches on, you might be driven to forget that the Lord was your life. I can tell you it's not like having *his* breath in your nostrils."

"Oh, my dear one," returned Janet with infinite tenderness, "I might indeed forget it! I'm sure I wouldn't be half so patient as you are. But I'll tell you what I would aim at. I would say to myself, if he is my life, I have no business with any more of it than he gives to me. I only have to take one breath, be it hard or easy, one at a time, and let him see to the next himself. And you might just think of yourself, Robert, that you're just new-born an old man, and beginning to grow young, and that that's your business. For neither you nor me can be very far from home, Robert, and when we get there we'll be young enough, I'm sure; and not too young, for we'll have what they say you can't get down here—old heads upon young shoulders."

"Well, I wish I could have you there with me, Janet, for I don't know what I would do without you. I would feel lost up there without you, the one who knows the ways of the place."

"I know no more about the ways of the place than yourself, Robert, although I'm thinking they'll be very quiet and sensible seeing that there must be fine people there. It's enough to me that I'll be in the house of my Master's father; and my Master was well content to go to that house. But poor simple folk like ourselves will have no need to hang our heads and look like fools that don't know manners. Babies aren't expected to know the ways of a great house that they've never been into in their lives before."

"It's not just that that troubles me, Janet. It's more that I'll be expected to sing and look happy and I don't know how it'll be possible with you not within my sight or my call or my hearing."

"Do you believe this, Robert—that we are all one in Christ Jesus?"

"I can't really say. I'm not denying anything the Bible tells me; you know me better than that, Janet. But there's many a thing in it that I don't know whether I believe on my own or whether it is only that a thing that you believe is the same to me as if I believed it myself. And that's a troublesome thought, for a man can't be saved by his own wife."

"Well, you're just where I am on that, Robert. I comfort myself with the hope that we'll *know* the thing there, that maybe we're just trying to believe here. We know that the two of us are one, Robert. Now we know from Scripture that the master came to make one forever those that were two; and we know also that he conquered death. So he would never let death make the one he had made one into two again—it's not reasonable.

"For all I know," Janet continued, "what looks like a parting may be coming nearer. And there may be ways of coming nearer to one another up yonder that we know nothing about down here. There's the boy Gibbie. I can't help thinking that if he could speak or make any sound with sense in it, like singing, say, he would find himself nearer to us than he can now. Who knows, but those who are singing up there before the throne may sing so pretty that their very songs may be like ladders for them to come down upon and place near loved ones they have left behind till the time comes for those to go up the ladders and join them in the green pastures about the tree of life."

More talk followed, but Janet's words about the power of song took such a hold of Gibbie that he stopped listening and fell asleep.

The next night Janet woke her husband.

"Robert! Robert!" she whispered in his ear. "Listen. I'm thinking there must be some small angel here come down to say 'I know you, poor folk.' "

Robert, scarce daring to draw his breath, listened with his heart pounding. From somewhere in the cottage came a low lovely sweet song—something like the piping of a big bird, something like a small human voice.

"It cannot be an angel," said Robert at last, "for it's singing the tune of 'My Mommy's Not Here'."

"Why no angel?" returned Janet. "Isn't that just what you might be singing yourself, after what you said last night? There must be a heap of young angels up there, newly dead, singing 'My Mommy's Not Here'."

"But Janet! You know there's no marriage in heaven."

"Who's talking about marriage? Is that to say we won't mean more to one another than other folk up there? Just because marriage is not the way of the country doesn't mean that there's nothing better to take its place!"

"What caused the Master to say anything about it then?"

"Just because they plagued him with questions. He never would have opened his mouth about it—it wasn't one of his subjects—if it hadn't been for a bunch of folk who didn't believe there were any angels or spirits of any kind. They said that a man once dead was then and forever dead, and yet pretended to believe in God himself anyway. They tried to confuse the Master by asking which of seven men a poor woman, who had to marry them all, would be the wife of when they came back to life."

"A body would think it would be left up to her to say," suggested Robert. "She had come through enough to have some claim to be considered."

"She must have been a really good one," said Janet, "if every one of the seven would be wanting her again. But I'm sure she knew well enough which one of them was her own. But, Robert, this is joking—not that it's your fault— and it's not fitting to joke about such a serious subject. And I fear . . . oh! there! . . . I thought as much! . . . The little song is stopped entirely, just as if a bird had gone to sleep in its nest. I doubt we'll hear any more of it."

As soon as he could hear what they were saying, Gibbie had stopped to listen, and now all was silent.

For weeks he had been picking out tunes on his whistle, the kind that used to be called Pan's pipes. Also, he had lately discovered that although he could not pronounce any word, he could imitate the pipes. Now, to his delight, he found his noises were recognized as song by his father and mother. From that time he often crooned to himself. Before long he began to make up tunes to fit words he came upon or poems he heard from Donal.

28
WORLDLY WISDOM

CHANGE, MEANTIME, WAS TAKING PLACE at the foot of Glashgar as well as in the little cottage high on its side—change which was to bring more changes. Thomas Galbraith hated superstition in others, but he had long ago fallen into the most degrading superstition of all—the worship of mammon, commonly called greed for money. And Thomas Galbraith was fully capable of being fooled by a lie. He risked not only his money, but his reputation for having good sense by investing in Welsh gold mines.

He was anxious to increase the size of his estate Glashruach, and so he repeatedly invested some money in hopes of gaining more money in order to buy more property. At last he had some success for the first time by selling some shares of stock for far more than they were worth. He didn't care if the buyer became poor as a result; he felt the glow of success. With his extra money he bought a small farm on good land between his home and the farmland of the Mains. He rented it right away to Farmer John Duff.

In the spring his finances weren't very good, so he went to London in May with his foolish idea that he had good business sense. There he fell into the hands of a member of parliament, whose true place would have been in a bunch of gangsters. This man was a friend of Thomas Galbraith's brother, another shady businessman, and between them they easily made Thomas Galbraith chairman of some "bubble" company that would soon burst and leave investors with nothing. Therefore, during the summer, he was in London promoting the company he half believed in himself, getting people to buy shares in it. This is the man who scorned simple folk because they believed in brownies. He had his own brownie in his head—foolish faith in false business.

During the winter Eunice, a sister of Donal's, was hired by the housekeeper to be a maid for Ginevra Galbraith. Ginevra was a dignified girl in whom childhood and womanhood were blending. How good it is when neither fully disappears in a person.

Eunice was the youngest of Janet's girls, about four years older than Donal, not clever, but as sweet and honest and godly as Donal. The moment she saw Ginevra's face she accepted her as a queen to serve and obey. Ginevra liked the healthy coloring and honest eyes of her maid, and before spring they were good friends. Ginevra was sometimes called Ginny, and Janet's daughter Eunice was always called Nicie. (She was named Eunice after the mother of St. Paul's friend Timothy in the Bible.)

One of Nicie's jobs was to accompany Ginevra to the home of the local pastor a mile and a half from Glashruach. There Ginevra had lessons from the middle-aged daughter of the pastor, Miss Machar. As she grew older Miss Machar had withered rather than ripening, and so she was not much of a teacher; but she taught Ginevra a little. For two years she had spent weekday mornings at Ginevra's house, but now her old father was ill and so Ginevra had to do the walking, with Nicie along.

29

THE BEAST-BOY

ONE MORNING THEY FOUND, on reaching the manse, that the minister was so ill that Miss Machar could not do any teaching. As they started to walk home to Glashruach, Nicie kept looking up the mountain toward where her parents' cottage was hidden by a ridge.

"What are you looking at up there?" Ginevra asked.

"I'm wondering what my mother's doing," answered Nicie. "She's up there."

"Up there!" exclaimed Ginny, and turned to stare, expecting to see Nicie's mother.

"No, you can't see her; she's not in sight. She's over beyond there. Only if we were up where you see three sheep against the sky, we could see the tiny house where she and my father live."

"How I should like to see your father and mother, Nicie!"

"Well, I'm sure they would be glad to see you any time you like."

"Why shouldn't we go now, Nicie? It's not dangerous is it?"

"No, Glashgar is as quiet and well behaved as any hill in the country," laughed Nicie. "She's rather poor, like many of us, and hasn't much to spare, but the sheep get a few nibbles upon her, here and there. And my mother manages to keep a cow and gets plenty of milk."

"Come, then, Nicie. Nobody will want us, and we shall get back before anyone misses us."

They began climbing the hill on a path Nicie did not know. After a while the path became unclear and seemed to split two ways.

"I'll take this way and you take that," suggested Ginevra, "and whichever one of us finds no path ahead will return here and follow the other." Nicie foolishly agreed and they parted.

Nicie soon saw that she was on the real path and sat down to wait for Ginevra. She waited in daydreams. Suddenly she realized that Ginevra was too slow in coming. She jumped up and ran back after her, calling in vain.

Ginevra thought she was on the right path and hurried as fast as she could toward the home of Nicie's parents. All she was following, however, was a mere sheep-track that led her finally into a lonely hollow in the hillside with a swampy peat-bog at the bottom of it. The place seemed dangerous. A lone-hearted bird uttered a single wailing cry that remained unanswered. With a pang of uneasiness Ginevra realized how alone she was. Ginevra was a brave child, and nothing frightened her much besides her father. So she retreated to the edge of the hollow to wait for Nicie.

Nicie, however, had accidentally taken a different sheep-track in her rush to find Ginevra, and they were far separated already. Far away down in the valley Ginny could see a tiny road with a tiny man in a cart pulled by a tiny white horse. She realized that no one could hear her if she screamed all day. Surely, she thought, Nicie would come soon.

But Ginny sat on a stone looking up the path so long that at last she began to cry. Ginny was very slow to cry, and it never relieved her sorrow. The tears would mount into her eyes and remain there like pools for a long time. At last when they had become two huge little lakes, two mighty tears would tumble over the edges and roll down her pale cheeks. This time many tears followed, and her lakes were becoming fountains.

All at once a verse she had heard the Sunday before at church came into her head: "Call upon me in the time of trouble and I will answer thee." It must mean that she was to ask God to help her. Ginny never thought much about God. She hadn't been taught much about him, especially not anything pleasant. Her soul was like a large wilderness ready for a voice to come to it crying to prepare the way of the King.

Ginevra knew she wasn't all good, and if God hears only good people, what was to become of all the rest when they were lost on mountains? It wouldn't do much harm to try to pray, even if God didn't listen. Only those who know Jesus pray to the real God, maker of our hearts. But God hears every honest cry anyway, in spite of our ignorance.

"O God, help me home again," cried Ginevra, and stood up and started walking back.

That instant she saw the beast-boy sitting on a stone near the path. His hair stuck out all over like a golden crown, and his arms and legs and feet were bare. He was playing sweet whistling music on something he held to his mouth. He was trying to catch her. Was this the answer to her prayers, that she would be killed and eaten by the monster? Apparently God was as harsh as they had warned about on Sundays in churches and in books Miss Machar made her read.

Ginny was the kind who was silent in terror rather than screaming. She sat down and stared, hoping he would go away. When that didn't work she started to run toward the swamp below in hopes of getting past him lower down the hill. She was willing to risk drowning if necessary.

Gibbie had been watching Ginny far longer than she knew. He had hoped she would get used to him. But as soon as she started to run he was after her and then ahead of her blocking her way to the water. She turned and started up a dangerous hill, and he appeared ahead of her. She threw herself to the ground and hid her face, waiting for him to pounce upon her and tear her to pieces like a lion. But nothing came.

She wondered if she could be dreaming. In dreams the hideous things usually never arrive. But she didn't dare to look up. Finally she heard a strange sweet voice singing, coming closer. Could it be an angel God was sending to save her? She opened her eyes and looked up. Over her stood the beast-boy! Or was it an angel in the shape of the beast-boy? No real beast-boy could sing so kindly or look at her with such blue eyes.

Then Ginevra had a strange miserable feeling connected with long ago, and she remembered the little child Angus had so cruelly lashed. If it was this boy, he might remember her. She *knew* this was the one, and smiled like dawn with stars in her eyes. Gibbie's face flashed like full sun in response, a smile no good person could mistrust. Ginevra took one hand out from under her cheek and Gibbie helped her get up.

"I've lost Nicie," she said.

Gibbie nodded with understanding. He knew Nicie very well.

Gibbie gave a shrill whistle and a dog came bounding to him over stones and heather. Ginevra didn't know what he told the dog or how he told it, but instantly it ran off along the path. Gibbie was so lively and expressive that Ginevra hardly realized he had not spoken. He took her hand and led her up the mountain. Her relief was so great and the hike up the mountainside was so exciting that she never for a moment felt tired. Then they went down the side of a stream whose dance and song delighted her; she learned later that it was the same stream she heard at night outside her bedroom window. They crossed the stream and climbed the opposite bank.

Then Gibbie pointed to the cottage, and there was Nicie climbing a path to the cottage with the dog bounding before her. The dog was happy but Nicie was weeping bitterly. Gibbie whistled, and Oscar came flying to him. Nicie looked up and came running like a sheep to her lost lamb.

"Oh Ginny," she panted, "what made you run away?"

"I was on a path and I thought you would come after me."

"I was a great goose, Ginny, but I'm glad I have you back. Come and see my mother."

"We'll tell her about it. I don't have a mother to tell, so we'll tell yours." From that moment on Nicie's mother was a mother to Ginny.

"Another of his lambs to feed!" Janet said to herself.

The moment Ginny was safe, Gibbie and Oscar ran off to care for the sheep. Ginny was having the happiest day of her life so far. She drank special milk and ate special oatcakes and listened to what they could tell her about Gibbie. She told them about the beating she had seen.

"Is he a good boy, Mistress Grant?" she asked.

"The best boy I ever knew," answered Janet. "Better than my own Donal, and he was the best before now. Nicie, have you seen Donal lately?"

"Not since I was here last," Nicie sighed.

"I was thinking he would come to see you now that he is working in the new meadow near the house where you work."

"Oh, is he there now?" asked Nicie. "Maybe I'll get to see him even if I'm not allowed to speak to him." Then she explained that Donal had come to the kitchen door to see her, but that Mistress MacFarlane, the housekeeper, wouldn't let him in. Nicie had explained that this was her brother, but the woman told her to shut her mouth, that no male visitors were allowed. Nicie had wanted to slap her she was so angry.

"She'll be sorry for it someday," Janet smiled, "so you might as well forgive her right now."

"How do you know she'll be sorry?"

"Because the Master says that nobody will do wrong without paying for it."

"But mightn't the Master forgive her?"

"Lassie," her mother said solemnly, "you surely didn't think the Lord's forgiveness is for people who don't repent? That would be a strange favor to people. He won't cause any unnecessary pain; but regret must make way for grace. That is why I had to spank you sometimes. But I must say I punished some of the older children when I didn't know so well what to do and I would get angry too easily. I still feel bad about that."

104

"Mother!" said Nicie, "Not one of your children thinks you ever did wrong."

"I dare say you're right. I think a woman's babies are like the God they came from—ready to forgive her for anything."

That gave Ginevra much to think about when she went home.

30

THE LORRIE MEADOW

DONAL GRANT LOOKED IDLE IN A FIELD tending cattle when he could
have been doing a man's work with horses on the farm. But he knew
well that such work would leave him no time for study. Therefore, with
his parents' permission, he kept his humble job with lower wages.

On the day following their adventure on Glashgar, in the afternoon,
Nicie suggested to Ginevra that they look for Donal in the meadow.
They made their way to the bank of the Lorrie.

"There he is!" cried Nicie.

"I see him," responded Ginny, "—with his cows all about the meadow.
I wonder what he is reading."

"That would be hard to say," answered Nicie. "Donal reads so many
books that Mother doubts he can well get the good of them."

"Do you think it's Latin, Nicie?"

"Oh, very likely. But no, it can't be Latin—for look! He's laughing,
and he couldn't laugh if he were reading Latin. I guess it is a story, or
indeed it may be a song. I heard my mother say once she was a bit
afraid Donal might end up writing songs himself. Not that there is anything wrong with writing songs, but they were hoping for something
important from Donal with all his book learning. Donal! Donal!"

Donal looked up and, seeing his sister, came running to the bank of
the stream.

"Can you come over, Donal?" said Nicie. "We want to ask you a question."

Donal was across in a moment, for here the water was only a foot or two deep.

"Oh, Donal! You've wet your feet!" cried Ginevra.

"What harm will that do me?" he laughed.

"None, I hope, but it might."

"I might have been drowned," said Donal.

"Nicie," said Ginny with dignity, "your brother is laughing at me."

"No, no," Donal apologized. "I was so glad to see you and Nicie that I was being silly."

"All right," said Ginny. "Would you mind telling me what book you were reading?"

"It's a book of ballads," he answered. "I'll read one to you if you like."

"I should like it very much," Ginny responded. "I've read all my own books till I'm tired of them, and I don't like Papa's books. And to tell the truth,"—here her voice grew sad—"I'm frightened to admit it, but I am very tired of the Bible, too."

"That's a pity," Donal replied. "I'd advise you to keep that secret because people who don't like the Bible a hair more than you do will condemn you for saying so. Just go up to my mother and tell her about it. She's fair to everybody and never thinks ill of people for telling the truth with good intentions. She says a lot of harm is done by people not saying what they think or know and trying to say what other people think instead."

"Yes!" said Nicie. "It would be a better world if people went to my mother and did what she said. She says people should tell their own faults and other people's good points; and that's just the opposite, you know, of what most people do today."

After a pause Ginny said, "I don't think you told me the name of the book you are reading, Donal."

"If you would like to sit down a minute," returned Donal, "I will read a bit to you and see if you like it before I tell you the name of it."

The two girls sat down happily to listen, and Donal read the ballad called *Kemp Owen.*

"I think—I think—I don't understand it," said Ginevra. "It is very dreadful. Tell me about it, Donal. Do *you* know what it means, Nicie?"

"Not a bit," answered Nicie.

Donal told them that it was the story of a lady who was turned into a serpent by a wicked witch. The witch twisted the serpent three times around a tree and laid a spell on her that until a knight kissed her three times she could not unwind herself from the tree and become a lady again.

"What a good, kind, brave knight!" said Ginevra.

"But it's not true, Ginny. It's only Donal's nonsense," Nicie objected.

"Nonsense or not, Nicie, it's not *my* nonsense. I wish it were. That ballad is hundreds of years old, I'm sure," answered Donal.

"It's *beautiful,*" said Ginevra. "I hope he married the lady and lived happy ever after."

"I don't know. The man that wrote the ballad thought him well paid if the lovely lady said *thank you* to him."

"But Donal, that wouldn't be enough! Would it, Nicie?"

"He only gave her three kisses—that wasn't much to do for a person."

"But a serpent!—a serpent's mouth, Nicie!"

Just then Donal had to rush after Gore, and the two girls decided it was time to go home. The rest of that day Ginevra talked mostly of the serpent lady and the brave knight and what a nice boy Donal was.

The next morning the girls returned to the brook and saw Donal and Gibbie together on the other side. The boys had their heads together over a slate upon which one and then the other would mark. This went on and on until Nicie called Donal. The boys sprang up and ran to the brook, but Gibbie stayed on the far side to guard the cows while Donal read to the girls for an hour without interruption. Nicie couldn't see why Donal and Ginny made so much fuss about old ballads.

After this the two girls went often to see Janet, and Ginevra learned much of the best from her. They also went often down to the Lorrie to see Donal.

Ginny's life was now the happiest it had ever been. Instead of learning less after losing Miss Machar, she was learning far more. She had new thoughts and feelings, new questions, and new interests. This was true learning.

Donal was soon devoted to Ginevra, and this enriched his own imagination. He thought Ginevra was as far above him in kind as she was in social class, and the only reason he got to associate with her, in his opinion, was that he was older and therefore knew a little more. He was so happy that he started to make verses for the first time.

One day, when Donal was reading from a book of Robert Burns to the girls, he tried out a poem he had made up. Gibbie, who was listening on the far bank, could guess from Donal's tone that these words were his own.

> Run, river, clatter
> Down to the ocean:
> If I were the water,
> How I would run!
>
> Blow, wind, cold and clean!
> Here and far below:
> If I were the wind,
> Wouldn't I blow!
>
> Shine, old sun,
> Shine on strong and fine:
> If I were the sun's son,
> Hearty would I shine!

Donal had hardly finished when Gibbie's pipes followed with a tune perfectly suited to the words. Donal knew that *one* listener had heard his poem well. But Ginevra had not appreciated it.

"That one is nonsense, Donal," she said. "How could a man be a river or the wind or the sun? Well, poets are silly. Papa says so."

Donal looked at the ground with his eyes; but with his mind he didn't know where to look. Luckily, at that moment Gore misbehaved. Gibbie knew what had happened to Donal, so he stayed in place and let Donal chase her. Instead of hitting the cow extra hard, Donal went easy on her because she had let him escape his audience. To have his first poem rejected this way was killing. The unkind criticism had come from a mere child, but she was the child he wanted to please. For a few minutes life seemed hardly worth living. He swore that he would never read another poem to a girl as long as he lived. But by the time he returned to Ginevra he knew what to say.

"Do you hear the stream after you go to bed?" he asked her. "What kind of noise does it make outside your window?"

"It is different at different times," she answered. "It sings and chatters in summer, and growls and cries and grumbles in winter."

"Do you think the stream is any happier in the summer?"

"No, Donal. The stream has no life in it and has no feelings."

"Well then, I'd like to ask how it's worse to pretend to be a stream than to imagine the stream a person, one time singing and chattering and the next time growling and grumbling."

"But Donal, *can* a man be a stream?"

"No, but didn't you ever imagine yourself running down with it—down to the sea?"

"No, Donal. I always imagine myself going up the mountain where it comes from and running about wild there in the wind when all the time I know I am safe and warm in bed."

"Well, maybe that's better; I couldn't say. But tonight, for a change, turn and go down with it in your thoughts. Listen and listen to it until you forget about yourself and feel the stream running, running, through this and through that, through stones and fern and heather and plowed land and woods and gardens, always singing and changing its tune till it winds to the great sea and enters it. And after that even if you don't wish you were a river at least you probably won't be so ready to find fault with the child that wrote that short little poem."

"Are you angry with me, Donal?" Ginevra asked anxiously.

"No, no. You're too good and too pretty to make anybody angry. But it would be disappointing to hear someone as special as you speaking like one of the folks who believe in nothing except what comes in at the holes in their head!"

Ginevra was silent because she couldn't quite understand Donal. But she suspected he was right, especially when she saw Gibbie's beautiful eyes full of admiration and brimful of love looking at Donal.

The way Donal kept his promise never to read another poem of his own to a girl was to make up a new one to read to her, as he lay awake that very night. He couldn't resist.

Ginevra became much more tactful in her responses to Donal's reading, and by degrees it dawned upon her that he wrote some of the poems himself. This turned Donal into a mystery and astonishment. Ginny could not imagine how it was possible to make verses, and this caused her to look at Donal with big eyes and a great new respect.

31
NICIE'S REWARD

GIBBIE BECAME A FAMILIAR SIGHT around the Mains. Angus scowled at Gibbie's smile but did him no further harm. Jean Mavor was friendly whenever Gibbie appeared with Donal. Fergus paid no attention to Gibbie and very little to Donal because Fergus was now a theology student and a fine gentleman. When Fergus came home with a master of arts degree he told Donal he should be more than a cowherd at his age. Donal smiled and said nothing. He was quite satisfied with a song he had just written that Fergus knew nothing about. Donal was not impressed by Fergus's career or his attitude.

In the autumn, Mr. Galbraith returned to Glashruach for a brief visit, eager to go on with his business schemes in London. He told Ginevra that since Miss Machar could no longer be her teacher he would soon send a new teacher to her from London. He had no idea that she was getting the best education possible for her age from Donal, Gibbie, and Nicie. He didn't want to know anything Ginevra might have liked to tell him, and so he didn't find out who her friends were and interfere. He never sent a teacher from London after all.

That winter fierce storms alternated with frozen calm, and for months Ginevra could not go to the cottage on Glashgar. After howling nights in which it seemed as if all the powerful ghosts of the universe were doing damage in the dark, the mountains stood solemn-still in the morning, each with a smooth white turban of snow on his head, in the profoundest silver-blue air, as if they had never in their life spent a more thoughtful, peaceful time than the past night. In all this time Ginevra did not see Donal or Gibbie.

At last the snow, like all other deaths, had to melt and run, leaving room for hope. Summer woke smiling as if she knew she had been asleep. The two young men and young women met again on Lorrie bank. The four were a year older, a year nearer trouble, and a year nearer getting out of it. Ginevra was more of a woman, Donal more of a poet, Nicie as nice as always, and Gibbie larger and stronger.

But Mr. Galbraith was so changed when he came home unannounced that Ginevra was shocked. The long thin man was now haggard and far more sour and suspicious looking. Instead of greeting Ginevra he turned his back to her and leaned against the mantelpiece. When she took his dangling hand in hers he let it droop lifelessly, which was worse than pushing her away.

"Is anything the matter, Papa?"

"I am not aware that I have been in the habit of communicating with you on the subject of my affairs," he answered coldly.

"I was frightened to see you looking so ill."

"Such a remark about my personal appearance is the kind of thanks I get for working myself to death to support you," he said bitterly. In fact he was planning to sell every foot of property Ginevra's mother had owned rather than holding it in trust for Ginevra. All his business schemes had failed. It had not dawned on him yet that his failure was due to mismanagement, not misfortune. He was a proud man, whose pride was always catching cold from his heart. He could have lived a hundred years with a child without learning to love at all.

He found so much fault with his servants that Joseph decided to look for another job. He scolded Ginevra so harshly that she began to hide from him. When he realized that she was avoiding him, he felt less guilty about selling all her dead mother's property, enjoying his insane idea that Ginevra was a wicked daughter. A conscience disobeyed becomes a cancer.

In this evil mood he got a message—Donal always believed it was from Fergus—hinting that Ginevra was a friend of the herd-boy at the Mains.

He was overwhelmed with disgust. He watched and waited, and at last one morning he saw the disgraceful girl sitting with her maid on the river bank listening to the cowherd reading to them, with the dumb idiot listening across the river. Enraged, he called Ginevra and in terror she went to him. He scolded her terribly and fired poor Nicie instantly. She had to leave without even a good-bye from Ginevra, weeping all the way home.

"You're welcome home, my pretty girl," said Janet, comforting her daughter. She knew that Nicie had done nothing wrong. And Nicie did not stay at home long, because Janet's children were known to be good workers and were in demand in the valley.

32

THE FLOOD

TOWARDS THE EVENING OF A BEAUTIFUL DAY in early August it began to rain. All the next day the slopes of Glashgar were alternately glowing in sunshine and swept with heavy showers; how often Gibbie was soaked and dried that day he could not have told. Late in the day the sun gave up and the wind became a hurricane. Gibbie drove his sheep into a sheltered pen and went home to tell Robert and to eat supper. Then he set out to climb the mountain. A great thunderstorm was at hand and was calling him. He always went to the top of Glashgar, when he could, if a thunderstorm was coming.

Lightning was like a rush of fire and the thunder followed in a series of single sharp explosions. Then wind and rain continued and the darkness was filled with the rush of water everywhere, wildly tearing down the sides of the mountain. To Gibbie these noises were a mass of broken music. He carefully found his way back to the cottage through the darkness and water, and in his bed he listened to the raging wind and rushing streams. When at last he went to sleep, he dreamed about the river of the water of life flowing from under the throne of God, and everyone who drank of it knew he was one with the Father and with every child of the Father in the entire universe.

Gibbie awoke with love in his heart and the sound of water in his ears. He dressed and opened the door to see the morning. A gray storm was

A great thunderstorm was at hand and was calling him.

all he could see, made up of rain and mist and steam and running water. On impulse he went back up the mountain. It looked to Gibbie as if the whole creation were crying for the Father and would not be comforted. Gibbie recalled how Jesus had gone to sleep in a boat in a storm and wondered why Jesus had been so tired. Then he figured out that healing people must have taken strength out of Jesus.

Just then Gibbie felt as if he were on a boat on the waves instead of on a mountain of stone, for Glashgar gave a great heave under him, then rocked and shook from side to side a little. The next instant there was an explosion followed by a spray of water and stones, and then a column of water was heaving out of a crack in the mountain-side and rushing and running downward as a large new stream.

Down the hill Gibbie shot, because this stream was headed toward the cottage. Before he reached home Gibbie had seen six or eight other new streams, and if he could have seen the other mountains he would have seen new streams there also. He wondered if a second flood of the whole world could be at hand, this time beginning in Scotland. Now and then a huge boulder would go rolling, springing after him like a hungry beast. And still the wind was raging and the rain tumbling down in sheets.

As he approached the cottage all he could see was a mass of water. To his amazement he found the cottage safe in the center of a water-fall that shot out from the great rock above it and sped on over bare rock where Janet's little garden used to be.

Janet greeted Gibbie joyfully. She, Robert, and Oscar were ready to go and had been waiting for him. Janet had on her best clothes and was carrying her big Bible, wrapped in a white scarf, and her umbrella. She gave Gibbie milk and muffins. Gibbie saw how damp the cottage was inside.

"What's the use of loading yourself with the umbrella?" Robert asked. "You'll get it all drenched. The wind is blowing too hard for it."

"Oh, I'll just take it anyway," Janet laughed.

"I bet you're taking it just to keep your Bible dry!"

Janet smiled and didn't deny it.

"Now Gibbie, you get Crummie," she said. "You'll have to lead her."

"Where are we going?" asked Robert. He trusted Janet completely.

"Oh, we'll just head for the Mains, if you don't mind, Robert," she answered. She led the way to the door and opened it. "His voice was like the sound of many waters," she said softly as they stepped out.

It was hard for the two old folk to walk all the way down to the Mains in a storm, but Gibbie was singing all the way and they chose to be content. Some of the raindrops felt like hailstones. After a while Janet decided that her umbrella was too much to carry. She tucked it close to a large rock and weighted it down with a few large stones, although Robert urged her to simply toss it aside.

"If I were troubled about saving my life," she said, "I could not share any thought for an old umbrella. But they both concern me so little that I may just as well look after them both." And the same umbrella, rescued later, served Janet to the day of her death.

33

THE MAINS

AT LAST THEY REACHED the valley road. Three days ago the Lorrie had been a lively little stream running and singing between grassy banks. Now it was flooded around the bridge to the Mains, and so there was nothing to do but wade on through. When they reached the yard, they sent Gibbie to find shelter for Crummie while they went into the house.

"The Lord preserve us!" Jean Mavor exclaimed when she saw them.

"He'll do that," Janet smiled.

"But what can God do?" Jean continued. "You've been flooded out of the hills, and what's to become of us in the valley? Oh my, you're wet!"

"Wet's not the word," said Robert, trying to laugh but too exhausted and asthmatic to get out even a chuckle.

Farmer Duff heard voices and came in.

"Hey, Rob!" he said as he entered. "I thought you had more sense. You were up the hill instead of down here by the river meadow. What brought you down here at such a ridiculous time?" He held out his snuff-box.

"Necessity, sir," answered Robert with spirit, taking a pinch of snuff.

"What necessity? Were you out of oatmeal?" the farmer retorted.

"Out of dry oatmeal, I'm sure," Robert said quickly. "You don't think Janet and I would be such old fools as to put on our Sunday clothes to swim in if we thought we'd see our home as we left it when we go back, do you? The foundation of the house is all I expect to see of it again. When the force of the flood grows less the water that's shooting over the house will probably crash down on it."

"Man! If the flood is above your house it was time to get out!"

After a change into dry clothes that Jean provided, the old couple was ready for some of her breakfast. But Jean wanted to know where her brownie was. His parents said he had been tending Crummie.

"Donal, send Dummy in to his breakfast," Jean called loudly across the yard.

"He went off to care for his sheep at home," Donal called back.

"Preserve us! He'll be lost!" Jean replied.

"Don't worry!" Donal yelled back, angry that she called his friend *dummy.* "Gibbie knows what he's doing better than those who think he's a fool just because he can't let out such stuff and nonsense as they can't ever hold in."

Jean came in fretting that Gibbie had no breakfast.

"He has a piece of bread," Janet said, "and that is what can be made more of. The Master himself fed thousands with a boy's five loaves and two small fishes. But I sometimes wish the Master had done it without anything to start with, so I could know how he would have managed."

"You're always wrestling with riddles," Jean said as she stirred the porridge hard. "Your curiosity might lead you far from the still waters some day."

"It's no problem," Janet answered calmly. "When Jesus says, 'What's that to you?' he doesn't have to say it twice. I get up and follow him."

This was beyond Jean, but she kept quiet because she had a deep conviction of Janet's goodness, although she took pride in her own superior common sense. In fact people who take pride in their common sense have a good deal more of the *common* than of the *sense.* Janet looked upon Jean as "an honest woman who'll get a lot of light someday."

120

After breakfast, Janet opened her Bible and Robert headed toward the barn to smoke his pipe, saying there was not much danger of fire that day. The rain fell, the wind blew, and the water rose. The fields were covered with yellow-brown water in which objects floated past the Mains, down the Daur to the sea.

"The land's just melting away into the sea. I can't see the good of it to anybody," Mr. Duff said at twilight as he dropped hopelessly into a kitchen chair. As evening closed in an elderly couple from a nearby cottage, and then the farm foreman's wife and children, came to spend the night in the safety of the big house. Yet Gibbie never came.

"There's one good thing," Robert said as he grew more worried. "Oscar is with him."

"Yes, Oscar has lots of sheep-care put into him," Janet added. "The one who made him, being a shepherd himself, knew what the dog needed." Robert knew that Janet was politely reminding him to trust God, not a dog. "Oscar's not with Gibbie," Donal said. "Oscar is outside here."

Janet stayed awake all night praying for her children. But she didn't call it praying. She called it keeping them company and holding the gate open.

In the morning Farmer Duff's heart sank within him. The clover field was gone and the sheep had moved to the watery corn field near the house. No one even expected Gibbie any more. It looked as if the only way to get to the Mains from anywhere was by boat. Yet after breakfast a strange, rough-looking woman knocked at the door. When Jean answered she stood and stared speechless.

"Great weather for ducks!" the woman said.

"Where did you come from and how did you get here?" Jean asked.

"I came from a ways away on my own two legs," she answered. In reality she had arrived the evening before and had slept in a barn loft all night, perhaps with a bottle of whisky. She looked like it.

"Your legs must be longer than they look, woman," Jean answered sharply. "You didn't come to the Mains to tell us about the weather!"

"If you could spare a glass of whisky—" the woman began.

"You'll get no whisky here!" Jean interrupted. "I would shut the door in your face if the weather were all right. I don't like your looks, but I have to let you in to save your life. You must behave because the farmer doesn't like tramps."

"I'll have you know I'm an honest woman and no tramp!"

"You shouldn't look like one then," Jean retorted.

Jean gave the woman a seat by the fire and oatcakes and milk. Janet kept knitting for Jean and said nothing, but now and then she cast a kindly glance out of her gray eyes at the woman. This stranger seemed like a lost sheep and aroused Janet's affection.

"She must be one my Master is seeking," Janet said to herself.

Some farm men tried to look for Gibbie but found it impossible. Robert had to quit going to the barn because it was becoming flooded, so he walked and prayed for Gibbie between Janet and the door. Janet prayed in her great trusting heart that if Gibbie were drowning or dying of cold, her God would be with him and hold his hand. To Janet life and death were small matters, but she was very tender over suffering and fear.

"It's a pity," Janet said to her restless husband, "that men don't learn to knit stockings or do other handwork. Many's the time my knitting is almost like a prayer closet for me, although I couldn't really go into it. But a prayer in the heart is sure to find the right road. Take courage. Maybe Gibbie will get here when you least expect him."

When the strange woman heard these last words a wild eager gleam lighted her face for a moment. Then she quickly looked blank again.

Still the rain fell and the wind blew. Wooden mills, thatched roofs, great mill wheels, went ripping and swaying and hobbling down. Houses were torn to pieces, and their contents were sent wandering on the brown waste through the gray air to the discolored sea. Chairs and tables, chests, carts, saddles, chests of drawers, tubs of linens, beds and blankets, work benches, cheeses, churns, spinning wheels, cradles, iron pots, wheel-barrows—all these hurried past the Mains. The water was now in the stable and cow houses and would soon be creeping into the kitchen.

Donal was out wading and came into the kitchen covered with mud, with a fresh rabbit in one hand and a big salmon in the other. "We're not likely to starve," he said, "with salmon in the hedges and rabbits in the trees!"

Just then the strange woman came in from the barn and announced that the stable would be washed away in another half hour. The farmer took a pinch of snuff and said that it would have to fall. At that the woman became angry and told him to take heart and get busy.

"You might at least give the poor horses a chance," she scolded. "I would rather drown swimming than tied by the head. But you have a dry place to put the horses. What are your floors like upstairs?" Her black eyes were flashing.

Gradually Mr. Duff understood her idea. The bedroom floors were strong enough to hold horses, and that great weight upstairs would make the house stand sturdier as the water pushed against it. There was no time to roll up the carpets, but horses are more valuable than carpets.

"The woman's right!" he cried as he shot from the house. Just as he entered the stable it began to fall apart. He called helpers and they led the horses through the water, splashing and stamping, and into the house and up the stairs. Mr. Duff led his favorite Snowball last of all, thinking that he would follow well. But the thundering of hoofs on the stairs added to Snowball's panic, and he broke away and plunged back into the stable. Duff darted after him and was just in time to see him rush out the far end of the stable into the water. Over and over he rolled in the deep current. Duff ran back into the house and looked out the highest window. He saw glimpses of his huge white horse swimming helplessly with the flood toward the Daur and the sea.

123

34
THE RESCUE

As soon as Gibbie had finished caring for Crummie he had rushed back to the Lorrie to cross the bridge just before it collapsed. Wading, swimming, walking on a wall, he made his way toward Glashgar, hidden by rain. A little way up the mountain he sat on a partly sheltered stone and pulled out the putty-like mass of wet bread and ate it gladly. He looked down at the valley flood and saw cattle drifting along, too tired to swim, their long horns knocking together like dry branches. He saw half a dozen helpless sponges of sheep floating along.

The sight of sheep set him off again on his treacherous zig-zag journey. He finally came to the pen where the sheep were now in danger of drowning. He opened the gate and drove them uphill a bit and left them. By now it was two in the afternoon and Gibbie was so hungry that he decided to see if by chance the cottage was standing with food in it.

Gibbie found the cottage standing and no longer under a huge stream of water. The water had apparently changed course soon after they left, because the house was not much wetter inside. Gibbie swept the floor and lit a fire and made himself some porridge. Then he sat in Robert's chair to dry off and fell asleep for an hour. When he woke up he took down the New Testament and began to read awhile.

Gibbie had tried reading parts of the letters in the New Testament a few times but hadn't understood them and was about to give up and return to the four Gospels. But now his eyes fell on some words in a letter from John that caught his attention and made him glad. He read until he came to these words in the third chapter: "Hereby perceive we the love of God, because he laid down his life for us; and we ought to lay down our lives for the brethren."

"How did John know that?" Gibbie asked himself. Janet had told him to try to see the teachings of Jesus as they showed up in the writings of his followers. At last Gibbie thought of his answer. Jesus had said, "This is my commandment, that ye love one another as I have loved you."

"And here I sit!" Gibbie realized. "Snug and rested with the world below in a flood. I can't lay down my life to save their souls, but I should save whatever I can for them, if only a hen or a calf."

Down the hill he went singing and dancing to where things might have to be done. He had no idea what he would do. Then he thought of his nearest neighbors at Glashruach and decided to go there first.

The front gate of Glashruach opened onto a bridge over the Glashburn. On the other side of the house, under Ginevra's window, a smaller stream ran down. Both of these fell into the Lorrie farther on. Gibbie hiked through larch and pine trees downhill toward the house set high between the two streams. He peered ahead through the rain. Where was the iron gate and its two stone pillars with wolf-heads on top? Where was the bridge? Where was the wall, and the gravel road to the house? Gibbie rubbed his eyes.

Below him was a wide, swift, fiercely rushing river that was gobbling up the ground on both sides. It was the Glashburn, fifty times its usual size. Foaming with madness, it roared along, rapidly drawing nearer the house as it grew wider. Slowly tall trees lowered their heads and sank into the torrent, and as soon as they touched it they shot away like arrows. Only now did Gibbie begin to fully realize the force of rushing water.

Mr. Galbraith was gone as usual, leaving Ginevra alone with Miss MacFarlane. There were no other servants in the house, but Angus had come into the kitchen to sit by the fire with Miss MacFarlane. He had been busy in the woodhouse all morning and had entered the kitchen by the back door and had no suspicion of what was going on in front of the house. He knew this was a severe flood, but he hadn't a notion how bad it really was.

This day had been the dreariest in Ginevra's life. Mistress MacFarlane had made herself so disagreeable that Ginevra stayed in her room to avoid her. She stood listlessly at her window looking out on the wild confusion of the storm. It was so loud that she didn't hear the gentle knock at her door, but she saw it softly open. There stood Gibbie! She imagined that he had come for shelter because his cottage had blown down.

"You mustn't come here, Gibbie," she said. "Go down to the kitchen, to Mistress MacFarlane. She will see what you want."

Ginevra knew that Mistress MacFarlane would be enraged if she saw them together, so she did not offer to go down. She looked back out the window instead. Then she gave a cry of astonishment. The stream below her window that had been wildly raging was suddenly almost dry. Instantly Gibbie knew what it meant. He snatched Ginevra up and ran with her down the stairs to the front door.

Ginevra had so much faith in him that she didn't struggle or scream. As soon as they were outside and she saw the Glashburn in her front yard, she understood part of the reason for his haste. She asked him to put her down and let her run beside him.

"Oh!" she cried, "Mistress MacFarlane! I wonder if she knows. Run and knock at the kitchen window." Gibbie obeyed at top speed.

As they crossed the empty stream bed it was obvious that a whole section of its bank had collapsed and made a huge dam. It was a fierce scramble in slippery mud and wild wind before they got up to high ground again on the far side of the empty stream bed. From there they had a grand view.

The dammed-up water swirled and beat and foamed against the

landlip, then rushed to the left, through the woods to the Glashburn into which it plunged. Rapidly it cut for itself a new channel. Every moment a tree fell and shot with it like a rocket. The stream came down the mountain as a white streak and burst into the boiling brown roar at Glashruach, full of branches and leaves and lumps of foam. Then Ginevra more fully realized the danger from which Gibbie had rescued her. The Glashburn was only about three feet from the front door of her house. But they couldn't watch any longer. The nearest shelter was the cottage, and Ginevra would need all her strength to get there. Gibbie took her hand.

"But where's Mistress MacFarlane?" she gasped. "We mustn't leave her." He replied by pointing. Miss MacFarlane and Angus were crossing the empty stream bed.

The climb they began would have been hard for any girl, especially for one who never got much exercise. What made it far worse was Ginevra's indoor shoes, which kept coming off. Gibbie did his best to tie her shoes on with strips of handkerchief and then finally ripped the sleeves off his corduroy jacket and tied her shoes on with strips from his sleeves. Her long hair was also a trouble; it kept blowing into her eyes and into Gibbie's too, sometimes with a sharp lash. But she never lost her courage. The excitement of battling the storm, the joy of adventure, and the pleasure of feeling her own strength sustained her a long time. Exertion kept her warm. Gibbie was so merry, fearless, and helpful that she hardly minded his silence. He carried her over the Glashburn at the only spot he thought it was possible to cross, and from there it was down-hill to the cottage.

Once inside, Ginevra threw herself into Robert's chair and laughed and cried and laughed again. Gibbie lit the fire and put on water and showed her where Janet kept her clothes. Then he rested on wet straw in the cow house. When he came back in, Ginevra was wearing Janet's work clothes and making porridge. She looked very funny. They ate supper in gladness and went to sleep.

Gibbie woke at dawn. The rain was falling in spoonfuls rather than drops. The wind came in long hopeless howls and shrill yells. Nature seemed in despair. There must be more for Gibbie to do in the valley.

Ginevra got up and Gibbie was not in the cottage. He had left a pot of fresh water, so she started the fire. Gibbie did not come. The water boiled. Several times she took the water off and put it back on because she was hungry. Gibbie never came. Finally she made herself some porridge. Then she found a slate on the table that said "I will come back as soon as I can."

It was dreadful to be left alone. She ate and then she cried. She felt unkindly treated, but she decided Gibbie was a sort of angel and had to go to help someone else. He had left her a little pile of books on the table, and she passed a couple of hours looking at them. But Gibbie did not return and the day passed wearily. She read and grew tired a dozen times; ate cakes and milk, cried afresh, and ate again. Here she was, one who had never yet acted on her own responsibility, alone on a bare mountainside in the heart of a storm that might go on forever. Not a creature knew where she was except the speechless boy, and he had left her. If the storm ended and she got down to the valley alone she might discover that no one else was left alive.

The noises were terrible. Through the general roar of wind and water and rain every now and then came a sharp crack followed by a strange low thunder. These were noises of stones grinding against each other and crashing into each other and falling and rolling. When it grew dark Ginevra could hardly bear her misery; but she soon slept the darkness away.

There was fresh light and hope in the morning. The rain was gentler, the wind had fallen, and the streams were not so furious. Ginevra ran to the stream for water to wash in and then put on her own clothes, which were now quite dry. Then she had breakfast and tried to say her prayers. But praying was difficult for her because she could not help seeing God like her father.

35
A LONG WET JOURNEY

A MOUNTAIN IN A STORM is as hard to cross as the sea. It took Angus MacPholp and Mistress MacFarlane hours to get the short distance to his cottage. There he stayed awake all night, peering out ever again into the darkness. When morning came the Glashburn was meeting the Lorrie in his garden. By breakfast time the water was behind the house also. When Angus saw water coming in at the front and back doors at once, he ordered his family upstairs. He stayed downstairs preparing fish nets to use after the flood, but when he found the water too deep he took his work upstairs.

There Mistress MacPholp stood at an open window holding her youngest child, a sickly boy, in her arms. He was holding a little terrier pup that his father valued greatly. In a sudden impulse of bad humor the child tossed the puppy out the window. It fell onto the roof and rolled off.

"Oh! The puppy's in the water!" Mistress MacPholp cried.

Angus threw everything down with an ugly oath, jumped up, and got out on the roof. He had given orders that the children were not to handle his puppy. Being a fair swimmer and an angry man, he threw off his coat and plunged after the dog, to the delight of his small son. He caught the pup with his teeth by the back of the neck and turned toward the house. Just then a shrub hit him in the face and caused him to blunder into the fast current, which bore him away. He dropped the pup and tried in vain to swim. He thought he was lost, and his wife screamed in agony. Gibbie heard her as he came down the hill looking for someone to help.

About a hundred yards from the house Angus was washed straight into a large elder tree. The weak branches were breaking, the flood was working at the roots, and any tree darting past in the current would carry this one away if they collided. Angus was not a man who could look with composure into the face of a slow, sure death. His own face was pale and terror-stricken, and that was the face that Gibbie saw from afar.

What could Gibbie do that would help Angus? If he could get a rope to him from the cottage that would be best. Gibbie caught hold of the eaves and scrambled out of the water onto the roof. But the woman wouldn't let him in the window. With a curse she had learned from Angus, she struck at him.

"You're not coming in here while my man's drowning there! Go to him, you coward!"

Never had Gibbie so much wanted to speak. He swam about and then crept back onto the roof. The woman saw him, grabbed a poker from the fireplace, and screeched at him from the open window.

Gibbie approached and she struck at him. He grabbed the poker, yanked it away from her, and jumped into the water with it. The next moment she could hear him breaking a window with it.

"He's coming to murder us all!" she cried, and the children screamed and danced with terror.

Gibbie was inside in a moment, seized a barrel, and attached it to a rope. He did that by breaking off part of a fishing rod, fastening the rope to it, slipping it into the barrel through the bunghole, and plugging the hole. He tied pieces of rope together until he thought he had enough length and tied the last piece to the fireplace. Then he pushed a few small pieces of furniture out the window to check the direction they would take.

130

Seeing her furniture float away, Mistress MacPholp began to scream. She thought that Gibbie was emptying her house in slow revenge, while her husband perished.

Gibbie floated out the barrel and swam along with it. It struck the elder tree and Angus yelled with joy. He clung to the barrel and kicked toward home while Gibbie swam his hardest to keep them away from the deadly current. Angus was so exhausted that it was all he could do to climb in the window, crawl upstairs, and collapse on the floor.

When his grateful wife went to look for Gibbie he was gone. Recalling how Gibbie had first released him from danger in Robert Grant's cottage and now saved him from drowning, Angus came to the conclusion that Gibbie was an angel sent from Satan. How should such a man imagine any other sort of angel taking an interest in his life?

In reality, Gibbie had a fresh thought after saving Angus. He emptied the barrel, which had a good deal of water in it now, and took out the stick. He plugged the hole again, wound fishnet all around the barrel, tied rope to the fishnet, and wound the rope around the barrel. Then he held the barrel and jumped back into the flood in order to swim down to the Mains. If he had wanted to do so he could have returned quickly to his home city, changing from one floating object to another as one after another went to pieces or sank. Once he saw a cradle come spinning along, and, using all his power, caught it. He hardly knew if he was more sorry or relieved to find it empty.

When he was about half way to the Mains, a whole fleet of hay ricks bore down upon him. He boarded one and scrambled to the top, hanging on to the rope that kept his barrel from floating away. From the top of the haystack he surveyed the wild scene. All was running water. A few roofs were visible, and the tops of trees were showing like low bushes. He drew near the Mains. All the hay ricks in the yard were bobbing about as if amusing themselves with a slow dance. So far the barn and the hawthorn hedge kept them from floating away.

131

Gibbie heard a horse's cry from far away. Surely it was a horse in danger! Then Gibbie recognized Snowball's voice. He stood up on the very top of his haystack to look through the wet air in the direction of the cry. Far away to the left he saw a speck of white that could possibly be Snowball on the turnpike road. Gibbie jumped off his haystack, rolled the rope around his barrel, and pushed off toward the cry. It took him a weary hour fighting currents. When at last he scrambled onto the embankment by Snowball the poor shivering creature gave a low neigh of delight. He did not remember Gibbie, but was glad to be with a human being. Gibbie tied the end of the rope to what remained of Snowball's halter and took to the water again. It was a long journey, and guiding the horse was much harder than swimming alone. Only someone much used to the water could have succeeded in such a trip. Along the way the barrel took in too much water and Gibbie let it go.

36

REUNIONS

JUST AFTER THE LOSS OF SNOWBALL a new family arrived at the Mains for shelter, floating in over the gate. The sight was hard to believe—a woman on a raft, with her four little children seated around her, holding her long skirt above her head and out between her hands for a sail. She had made the raft herself by tying some fence posts together and crossing them with what other bits of wood she could find. Nobody knew her. The farmer was so struck with admiration for her cleverness and courage that he decided to keep the raft as a souvenir. He couldn't bring it into the house, so he tied it to one of the windows.

When they had the horses safe on the second floor, they brought the cows into the lower rooms. But it was soon obvious that if the cows were to survive they would have to be upstairs. That caused such a tumult, such a banging of heads and hindquarters, of horns and shoulders, against walls and partitions, such a rushing and thundering, that the house seemed more in danger from the animals inside than the water outside. The cattle behaved worse than the horses. One poor cow broke both her horns off against the wall at a sharp turn in the hall. The men tried to rush the cows too much, so Donal asked the farmer to let him and his mother care for the cows because Janet had a wonderful way with them. When Gore's turn came and Donal began to tie ropes to her hind hoofs, Mr. Duff objected. But

133

Donal explained that she would gore and kick if she had the chance and that upstairs there would be no space to whack her without hurting other cows. Mr. Duff decided to let Donal do as he pleased, and he and Janet got Gore safely in place with her horns and back legs secured so that she could only bellow and paw with her forefeet.

The humans were mostly in Fergus's bedroom, the horses were in his father's, and the cows were in the other bedrooms. Mr. Duff acted fairly calm, but he was nearly at his wit's end. He would stare out a window for half an hour murmuring now and then, "This is clean ridiculous!"

The strange woman sat in a corner very quietly. There was altogether more water than she liked. Her eyes shot flame in the afternoon when Jean brought in the whisky bottle to give everyone a drink. Jean poured out a glassful, took a sip, and offered it to Janet. Janet didn't want any. Then Jean offered it to the strange woman. She took it casually, swallowed it with one gulp, and gave the glass back for more. Jean glared into her greedy eyes and filled the glass for the mother who had built and sailed the raft. The strange woman muttered something like a curse upon skimpy servings and drew farther back into the corner.

"I suspect we have an Achan in the camp—a Jonah in the ship!" Jean said to Janet as she turned to carry the bottle and glass from the room. She obviously meant that the strange woman would bring them bad luck.

"No, no," replied Janet. "Folk that's not been guided right, not knowing where their help lies, sometimes take to the bottle. But this is not a day of judgment for wrong doing, and I think the worst is nearly over. If only Gibbie were here!"

After Jean left the room the strange woman put her hand on Janet's arm, looked into Janet's soft eyes with her hard ones, and said, "You have more than once made mention of one connected with you by the name of Gibbie. I knew a Gibbie long ago that was lost sight of."

"There's Gibbies here and Gibbies there," Janet answered guardedly.

"Well, I know," she answered crossly and turned away, muttering so that Janet could hear, "but there's not many little Sir Gibbies, or the world wouldn't be so much like hell."

Janet wondered if this fierce, unfriendly, whisky-craving woman could be the mother of her gracious Gibbie. Could she be, and look so lost? But the loss of her son could have caused her to lose her self, perhaps.

"How did you come to lose the boy, woman?" she asked.

"He ran from the bloody hand," Mistress Croale answered carefully. She had no intention of giving any information to Janet.

"How did he get the nice nickname?" Janet finally asked.

"Nickname!" retorted Mistress Croale fiercely. "His own name and title by law and right, as I have often heard his father, Sir George, say so."

"You wouldn't be his mother, would you?" Janet asked. There was no answer.

"Would you know him if you saw him again?" she tried.

"Know him? I'd know him if he had become a grandfather. Know him, she asks! Anyone who knew him as I did, baby that he was, would know him if he were dead and turned into an angel! But it doesn't matter now!"

She was upset and went to look out the window.

"What was it about him you would know so well?" Janet asked in a tone of indifference. It was clear that this woman knew more about Gibbie than she was willing to tell, and she worried Janet.

"I'll know those that ask me before I answer," she replied sullenly. But the next instant she screamed, "Lord God Almighty! There he is!" and in her excitement she dashed a hand into the window pane, cutting her wrist.

At that moment Jean entered and heard the cry and the breaking glass.

"Get away from the window, you rude beggar!" she exclaimed.

Mistress Croale didn't notice. She stared from one window and

Gibbie, like a Triton on a seahorse, came through the water on Snowball.

Janet stared from the other as Gibbie, like a Triton on a seahorse, came through the water on Snowball. Jean went to Janet's window and saw the triumphal approach of her brownie, saving the lost Snowball.

"John! John!" she called. "Here's your Snowball!"

John was beside himself with joy, and from all the windows Gibbie was welcomed with shouts and cheers and congratulations.

"Lord preserve us!" cried Farmer Duff when he realized quite late who the rider was. "It's Rob Grant's moron! Who would have thought it possible?"

"The Lord's little ones are very capable sometimes," Janet said to herself. She believed Gibbie was smarter than her own children, Donal included, and she did not believe the popular idea that brains and heart don't come in the same person. In her own case she had found that her brains were never worth much to her until her heart took up the education of them.

Everyone shouted questions and advice to Gibbie at once, and he replied to them all with a radiant smile. When he and Snowball arrived at the door they found a difficulty. The water was so high that Snowball's head was above the door lintel; and, though all animals can swim, they do not all know how to dive. Everyone had suggestions. But Donal had already joined Gibbie in the water and the two had a plan. They fastened a rope around Snowball's body and gave the end to Janet, who stood on the stairs. She was to pull Snowball inside as soon as he went underwater. Donal threw his arms around Snowball's neck from below and pulled down just as Gibbie pushed with all his weight from above. The next thing Snowball knew he was indoors. As he scrambled heavily up from the water Farmer Duff and Robert seized him and patted him and led him to the bedroom to the rest of the horses. There he started eating hay from his master's bed. When Gibbie came upstairs he was seized by Janet, embraced like one come alive from the grave, and led dripping into the room where the women were.

The farmer came right in with a glass of whisky for Gibbie; it was their all-purpose medicine. But Gibbie turned from it with a curious look of gratitude and disgust. The sight and smell of whisky were horrible to Gibbie. His father's life had not been all failure; he had passed on to his son what he had learned through experience. Not many parents accomplish that.

As the farmer left the room Gibbie danced around Janet and balanced on one leg in joy. Farmer Duff thought Gibbie was making merry in spite of other people's trouble because he had nothing to lose and didn't understand. It didn't occur to him that Gibbie's joy came from saving his own lost horse.

"He's a born idiot," he told Jean afterwards, "and it's just a marvel what he can do anyway! But there's not much to choose between him and Janet. They'll both do well enough in the next world, I suppose, where nobody has to take care of themselves."

When Janet learned from Gibbie that her cottage was safe she felt that she had lacked faith when she left home. If she had stayed there she could have seen the miracle when God turned the water aside. She was ashamed.

When Janet looked for Mistress Croale in her corner the woman was gone. In fact she had slipped out of the room when Mr. Duff left, and no one had noticed. Just then some cows had got excited and he had hurried to them, leaving the whisky bottle on a chair in the hall. When she saw the bottle abandoned within her reach she was exalted with delight. It was the key of the universe to her. She put the bottle to her lips and drank. But she thought while she drank and did not drink more than she could handle. Noiselessly she set the bottle down, darted into a tiny room that held one calf, and stood looking out the open window. The raft was attached to that window.

At suppertime she was missing altogether. The conclusion was that she had fallen out a window and drowned. The farmer checked the windows and saw the raft was gone. A hired man recalled that an hour

138

earlier he had seen what he thought was a large dog floating downstream on a big door; it must have been the strange woman floating away on the raft. Because she was gone and the raft was gone, they probably went together, incredible as it seemed. No one believed she could have gone very far before she drowned.

Farmer Duff said the weather changed with the return of Snowball; his sister said it changed with the departure of the tramp. Before dark the rain had ceased and the water had stopped rising. In two hours it sank a quarter of an inch.

Gibbie slept all night beside his mother's chair. At dawn he woke up from a dream that Ginevra was in trouble and hurried off to care for her. He made it clear to Janet that he would return soon to guide her home. In the afternoon he did that, although it was a long, roundabout journey. It was night before Gibbie and Janet arrived at their cottage, which Ginevra had made warm and tidy. It was heavenly bliss to Ginevra to hear their approaching footsteps. She had learned that the poorest place where the atmosphere is love is more homey and more heavenly than even the most beautiful place where law and order rule.

From that day forth, for about a year, the house at the Mains was filled with a slowly subsiding flood of Jean's complaints about the harm that the water had done to their possessions. When her brother pointed out that most of the items she lamented over were still good and that this was not a major tragedy, she answered that he would complain more than she did if Snowball had not been rescued for him. It was probably true. Farmer Duff never thanked Gibbie for saving Snowball; an idiot wouldn't understand thanks. He never considered giving Gibbie a reward; what use was money to him? But he always spoke kindly to Gibbie from that time on, and Gibbie felt well thanked and well rewarded.

37

THE INHERITANCE

WHEN GIBBIE DISAPPEARED FROM THE CITY many people became interested in his fate, and Clement Sclater gathered all the information he could find about Gibbie's family and history. He located a second cousin of Gibbie's mother, who had inherited the family home. This man had no interest in Gibbie at all, claiming that Gibbie's mother had disgraced him and his relatives by her poor marriage. He acted as if he took pride and satisfaction in being disgraced that way. The more completely the orphan disappeared, the better it would be in this man's opinion.

There was also a bachelor brother of Gibbie's mother still alive—William Fuller Winthrop, the senior partner in a large ship-building firm. His reputation didn't offer Mr. Sclater any hope. He believed that man was made neither to rejoice nor to mourn, but to possess. Waste was so wicked to Mr. Winthrop that any other risk was preferable. Mr. Sclater wrote to him anyway, just in case. Mr. Winthrop replied that since his sister had been disowned long ago it would be improper for him to take any interest in helping her child. Out of curiosity, he said, he had once inquired about the boy and learned that he was little better than an idiot, who picked up his character, education, and manners in the street. He was sure that anything done for such a child would only make him more miserable and wicked.

At that point, Mr. Sclater felt he had done all that was required of him as minister to the parish where Gibbie had lived. It could not be his duty, he thought, to spend time and money in hunting a boy whose home had been with the dregs of society. Of course Mr. Sclater did not know Gibbie, even by sight, and wouldn't have known what to do with him if he had found him.

One morning at breakfast with his wife, who had been the Widow Bonniman, he read in the newspaper that William Fuller Winthrop had suddenly died. He held his coffee cup halfway to his lips while he read the facts. Then he put the coffee down untasted and rushed from the room. In fact, he put the cup down on its side and made a mess of the table and upset his wife with his unexplained rudeness. That was because Mr. Winthrop had left no will when he died and had left two hundred thousand pounds. It was obvious that Sir Gibbie was the legal heir if he could be found.

Sir Gibbie was still considered an idle tramp; but now he was an extremely rich idle tramp, and that made all the difference to Mr. Sclater. He went right to his lawyer about the matter and then would have gone to Mistress Croale for information if he could have found her. But he had been far too successful in chasing her out of his parish.

Mistress Croale had become a drunkard and then a wanderer, and where she went she sold small items like scissors and pins to housewives. Sometimes they bought from her because she seemed evil and rather frightened them. The real cause of the bad impression she made was not that she was evil, but that she had what is called a bad conscience. That is a good conscience that does its duty well and makes its owner uncomfortable.

She heard the astounding news that Gibbie had inherited a fortune and that there was a reward of a hundred pounds for anyone who gave information that led to his location. His description was made public, and he was such a conspicuous boy that Mistress Croale felt she would have to move fast to get the reward. She had as a clue the fact that Sir George used to talk about property on Daurside. She filled a basket with little things to sell and wandered around Daurside looking for Gibbie, but afraid to ask. Then in the great flood she made her discovery and hurried back to the city. Some of those who recalled her in the valley were of the opinion that she and the flood were closely related and both sent by the devil.

38

LEAVING GLASHGAR

JANET AND GIBBIE WENT RIGHT AWAY to the Galbraith home in case anyone was there who needed to know about Ginevra, but all they found was a ruin in the wilderness. Acres of trees and shrubbery had disappeared, and what was left of the house stood on a red gravelly precipice fifty feet high. Not a sign of life was about the place; the very birds had fled. Angus had been there that morning and locked or nailed up every entrance. It looked like a ruin of centuries.

When Angus and the housekeeper had heard Gibbie's taps at the window and saw how close the stream was, they had fled for their lives. They never knew who had tapped to save them. As she passed the foot of the stairway Mistress MacFarlane shrieked to Ginevra to come, and that was all she did for her. Thinking the girl had perished, the two claimed that they took Ginevra with them and that when she disappeared they returned to the house to look for her and were themselves almost drowned. They made themselves out to be heroes instead of selfish cowards. Mistress MacFarlane had been extremely harsh to the maids about lying, but when she could gain by it she lied like an expert.

Ginevra immediately wrote letters to her father in London, but he never got them. Then she had days of freedom and delight with Gibbie on Glashgar. He never hurt anything, and nothing ever

143

seemed to hurt him. And what a number of things he knew! He was always out with his sheep hours before she was up, and when she joined him he was often seated on a stone or lying in the heather reading his pocket New Testament. The moment he saw her he would spring up merrily to welcome her. This was a boy with a hearing ear, a willing heart, a ready hand.

On the fourth day the sun was glorious, and Ginevra asked Gibbie to take her to Glashruach to see the ruin. She would not have recognized the property or the house. They entered a door that used to be inside, but was now on the outside. There was sand in the hall. The dining-room was a miserable sight. The thick carpet was spongy like rain-soaked moss, the leather chairs looked diseased, the color was gone from the table, the wallpaper hung down loose, and everything lay where the water had dropped it.

They went up the old stone staircase and walked across her father's study to look out the window. His study was in perfect order. Suddenly Ginevra saw her father standing at the window; she turned pale. Gibbie saw that she was afraid of her father and thought how good his own dear father Robert was.

The lord turned and saw Gibbie and waved at him to get out. Then he saw Ginevra's pale face and thought she was a ghost; he had been told she must be dead. The secret memory of that moment disgraced him forever in his own eyes because it showed that his disbelief in ghosts was not perfect. As he stood frozen in fear Ginevra walked toward him and said in a trembling voice, as if she expected the blame for the entire flood, "I couldn't help it, Papa."

Overcome with relief as well as sorrow, he took her in his arms and kissed her. She clung to him in warm response. But he straightened up and saw Gibbie standing there smiling at the happy scene.

"Leave this house instantly," he said, "or I will knock you down."

"O Papa!" Ginevra begged, "don't speak so to Gibbie. He's a good boy. He saved me from drowning in the flood. He's the one Angus whipped long ago and almost killed."

"If he doesn't leave fast I'll have him whipped again. Angus!"

Ginevra cried out in horror and Gibbie sprang to her side to comfort her. Her father seized him and threw him across the room. He fell backward, his head striking against the wall. Angus entered, and when he saw Ginevra he gasped in terror and yelled and his hair stuck out as if electrified.

Gibbie saw that his presence made things worse for Ginevra, so he walked out. To comfort her he sang loudly to her from a distance as he left.

"What do you know of that fellow, Angus?"

"He's the very devil himself, sir," Angus muttered.

"Then make sure the scoundrel leaves and never returns."

Angus was glad to get away from Ginevra's presence.

"So, Ginny!" her father said, with his loose lips pulled out straight, "this is your choice—a low, beggarly, insolent scamp!—scarcely the equal of the brutes he has charge of!"

"They're sheep, Papa!" Ginevra wailed.

"This girl is an idiot," he said dramatically, turning his face away in contempt.

"I'm just an idiot," she agreed. "Let me go away and I'll never bother you any more." She wanted to become a mountain shepherdess with Gibbie. She knew that Janet would take her in.

In answer her father grabbed her by the arm, pushed her into a closet, locked the door, and left her there while he ate lunch. That afternoon he left with her for the city, where he meant to place her in a girls' school.

Gibbie knew that Ginevra had stepped from day into dark, and he went home sad. He comforted himself with the knowledge that Ginevra had another father besides the lord of Glashruach.

When he reached home he saw that Janet was crying; but she was calm and dignified as usual, although her cheeks were wet.

"Here he comes!" she had said to a visitor as Gibbie entered. "The will of the Lord be done—now and forevermore! I'm at his bidding, and so is Gibbie."

The visitor was Mr. Sclater. Mistress Croale had successfully earned her reward.

39

JOY IN THE CITY

ONE BRIGHT AFTERNOON toward the close of autumn a procession of school girls was being led down a wide clean stone street, two by two in a long file. The girl walking by the teacher had lovely brown eyes, trustful and sweet, sad but shining. Suddenly an odd-looking boy burst into the line and held her daintily gloved hand and laid a hand upon her shoulder. The outraged teacher, Miss Kimble, poked at the boy with her parasol and tried to shoo him away in vain.

Then the minister Mr. Sclater rushed up and put his hands on the boy's shoulders to draw him away from the prey he had pounced on. He was greatly embarrassed.

The girl, whose cheeks were pink and whose eyes were wet, said, "Gibbie and I are old friends." She put her hand on his shoulder as if to protect him. Her teacher was horrified.

"Pray do not alarm yourself," said Mr. Sclater. "This young . . . gentleman is Sir Gilbert Galbraith, my ward. He is going to study with me for a while before going to college."

"Oh!" Miss Kimble said. "I'm glad to hear it. I hope I did not hurt you with my parasol. A relative, Miss Galbraith! I did not understand."

Gibbie laughed, and a strange smile began to play about Ginevra's sweet strong mouth. All at once she was in the middle of a fairy tale. Her dumb shepherd boy was a baronet and a Galbraith! The last she

147

had seen of Gibbie was as he was driven from the ruined house by her father.

Mr. Sclater had taken gentle pains to convince the old couple that they must part with Gibbie. Once he brought a neighboring pastor who knew him well to assure them that Mr. Sclater had become Gibbie's legally appointed guardian. Another time he brought Fergus Duff to tell them so. It was obvious to them that unless something like what he said was true Mr. Sclater wouldn't want Gibbie at all.

The main difficulty was Gibbie himself. He laughed at the idea of going away. They told him he was Sir Gilbert Galbraith. He answered that he had told them that fact long ago. "And what differs dos that mak?" he wrote on his slate.

Mr. Sclater told him he would become a rich man some day. "Writch men do as they like, and I'll stay here," Gibbie answered.

Mr. Sclater told him that only poor boys can do as they please. The law looks after boys who will someday be rich so that they can learn to use their money properly. Gibbie went out and stayed part of the night on the crest of Glashgar. He would like to help people. When he came back he wrote on his slate:

> "my dear minister, If you will teak Donal too, and let him go to the kolledg, I will go with you as soons you like—butt if you will not, I will runn away."

When Mr. Sclater read the slate the next morning he shook his head in bewilderment over the problem of taking *two* savages home to civilize. That instant Gibbie darted out of the house. Mr. Sclater's blunder had caused him to lose another day. He consulted Janet about what to do. She told him that Donal was her own son and that he would be visiting that very evening and then the minister could judge for himself. Mr. Sclater was well pleased with Donal when he met him and even more pleased when Janet said that Donal should live in a small rented room in the city rather than at the Sclater home with Gibbie. So Gibbie's money enabled Donal to go to college that autumn.

Mr. Sclater saw the job of guardian as a great deal of trouble, but it put him in command of some money and would eventually give him influence over large wealth. His wife's property had already made him somewhat rich, and he was eager to increase his power further. This job was a long-term investment.

When Gibbie met Miss Kimble and her girls, he was on his way to the Sclater home for the first time. He was full of joy. How well he knew every corner on Daur Street. What happy days he used to have there with all the hunger and adventure! The Master was in these city streets as certainly as on the rocks of Glashgar. Not one sheep did he forget.

40

MEETING MRS. SCLATER

MR. SCLATER STOPPED AT A LARGE and important looking house, with a flight of granite steps up to the door. Gibbie had never been inside such a house in his life, except for a glimpse into Glashruach, but he was not much impressed. He followed Mr. Sclater up the stair with the free mounting step of the Glashgar shepherd. Mrs. Sclater rose when they entered the drawing-room, and Gibbie approached her with a smile of welcome to his heart. She shook hands with him in a doubtful kind of way.

"How do you do, Sir Gilbert?" she asked. "Only ladies keep their caps on in the drawing-room, you know."

Gibbie didn't even know what a drawing-room was. Suddenly he remembered that he had a cap on. He knew that men took hats off indoors, but he had never done it before because he had never owned one. He smiled with amusement, put the cap in his pocket, then sat on a small footstool and looked around the room while Mr. Sclater gave his wife a very dull account of their trip.

Gibbie looked at things in the room with no idea that they gave a sense of great superiority to their owners. To Gibbie every human was sacred, even a beggar. Likewise, to Gibbie a clay floor and a rich carpet were much the same. To him this cluttered house was less charming and less comfortable than the cottage on Glashgar, but it was a home for people and so he liked it. He could enjoy its stateliness and many colors and variety of details.

Mr. Sclater had gladly moved into this elegant house when he married Mrs. Bonniman, whose first husband had earned his wealth in foreign trade. She was slowly polishing Mr. Sclater and training him in the small duties and graces of social life, and he embarrassed her sometimes with his clumsy behavior and ignorance. It was natural for her to dread the same kind of thing in far greater degree from Gibbie. She told her friends that she didn't much care to become a mother to a bear-cub.

"Just think," she said, "with such a childhood as the poor boy had, what a mass of vulgarity must be lying in the uncultivated brain of his! It's no small mercy that at least our ears are safe! Poor boy!"

She was a tall woman, about forty, with a rosy face, shiny black hair, and fine white teeth—a very handsome woman. She always wore satin dresses. Everything in her house was "in good style" although she did not have truly good taste. She was particular about everything, but kind and reasonable to the servants. She was seldom in the wrong and never admitted it when she was, but when she saw her mistake she always avoided making that mistake again. She was an ideal wife for the middle-aged Mr. Sclater, and it would have been hard to find anyone who could do more to teach Gibbie to be a gentleman.

As she contemplated Gibbie, his blue eyes met her black ones and then light rushed in like a torrent and broke into an extraordinary smile. From that moment on the lady and the shepherd boy were friends. She told friends the next day there was something in his smile no woman could resist, and it must have been inherited from his family line. If she had seen some members of his family line she would not have thought they had anything to do with his smile at all.

Gibbie began to examine Mrs. Sclater with his innocent eyes until she became very uncomfortable, although she didn't know why. She didn't think he was rude, but she wished he would stop it. Then he became fascinated by her graceful soft white hands that lay in her black satin lap. He moved his little stool across the hearth rug next to her and put one of his hands on hers and broke out laughing. She laughed also—who could have helped it? His laugh would have set silver bells ringing in response. She patted the lumpy thing that was his hand. It was hard, brown, stained dark in the creases, with uneven black fingernails. Her lovely long fingers were adorned with a limpid activity of many diamonds and her wrist was hooped with blue-green turquoises. Gibbie obviously admired the beauty of her hand, and she knew his likes and dislikes told much about his character. Nevertheless, Mrs. Sclater was glad when her husband took Gibbie to his room to get ready for dinner.

Within a few hours she began to suspect that she felt less satisfied with herself when Gibbie's blue eyes looked at her. She led a tidy, respectable life and had done almost nothing wrong. But no human consciousness can be clean until it lies wide open to the eternal sun and the all-powerful wind of God. Then the dim cellar of the mind becomes a mountain top. Mrs. Sclater needed to learn from Gibbie more than he needed to learn from her.

41

AN EAGER PUPIL

MRS. SCLATER'S FIRST PROJECT the next morning was to take Gibbie to the most fashionable tailor in the city and have him measured for fine clothes. Gibbie was wearing a suit of clothes that Mr. Sclater had bought him in the village near Glashgar, and it was an awkward, ill-fitting suit. Gibbie could endure cold or wet or hunger and sing like a bird. He had borne pain bravely. But tight arm-holes were different.

Suddenly Gibbie darted away from Mrs. Sclater and crossed Pearl Street pulling off his jacket. On the other side he stopped a boy his size who was dressed in rags and held the jacket for him to put on, with all the attentive flourish of a salesman. The boy nodded in gratitude and hurried away before anyone would make him give back the jacket. He assumed that Gibbie was insane. Mrs. Sclater watched with amused concern, not minding the loss of such a poorly made jacket, but wondering if Gibbie was in his right mind after all. Gibbie went along with her, swinging his arms in relief.

Mrs. Sclater soon began to find that in learning good manners Gibbie was the best possible pupil. She was quite proud of the power she seemed to have over the young savage; she had not yet discovered that Gibbie was in control. He liked her refinement and was eager to learn better ways of doing things, but he had no intention of obeying her unless he saw fit. Neglected in childhood and absolutely trusted by his mountain parents, he had no idea of obedience to anyone except Jesus.

Mr. Sclater did his duty. He was a sensible teacher and soon discovered how to work with Gibbie's writing ability. Gibbie had already started to learn Latin from Donal, and he made such good progress with Mr. Sclater that after a while the minister wished that half the students and church members were as silent as Sir Gilbert Galbraith. When he started to teach Gibbie Greek, they were hardly past the first verb when Gibbie became fascinated with the Greek New Testament.

42

DONAL'S NEW HOME

Donal had to stay at the Mains for a couple of weeks after Gibbie moved to the city, waiting for a new herd-boy to take his place. He spent his last night with his parents, then started off in morning moonlight to catch the coach to the city. His trunk with his few possessions in it had already arrived from the Mains. Jean had put in as a surprise for Donal a cheese, a bag of oatmeal, some oatcakes, and two pounds of the best butter in the world.

Mr. Sclater met Donal at the coach office and hired a porter with a wheelbarrow to take Donal and his trunk to his new address. He said Sir Gilbert would visit the next day, and he went on his way.

The porter and Donal walked to Widdiehill and the porter found the address he had from Mr. Sclater. They went through a furniture shop, up dark stairs, and through a dusty storage area to the rented room that would be Donal's home. It was bright and cheerful, with a fire going and tea things set out. Donal felt alone and sat down to warm himself. All of a sudden Gibbie jumped out from behind the curtains and threw his arms around him.

The boys had a jolly time of it. They made their tea and ate heartily. Gibbie found a bell-rope and rang for Donal's landlady, a woman he had known in his childhood. She chattered as she removed the tea tray. Suddenly she stared hard at Gibbie. His hair was newly cut, his shirt was the whitest linen, his tie was the richest of black silk, his clothes were the latest style, and his boots perfect. The landlady knew him anyway, and she was so excited that she stayed for an hour. She answered many of Donal's questions, but whenever he asked about Gibbie's family she pretended she hadn't heard. Then Gibbie looked a little sad and thoughtful.

When the good woman left, they unpacked Donal's trunk, discovering Jean's gifts, and arranged everything. Then they sat down to read, and time passed quickly.

At about ten o'clock Mr. Sclater walked in without knocking. Gibbie sprang up with a smile. But Mr. Sclater was furious because of what he called vulgar and ungentlemanly behavior in the middle of the night. It didn't matter to him that the boys had been sharing a good book. Gibbie had been away from home for hours without permission. Mr. Sclater stormed on and on; Donal glowered into the fire; and Gibbie stood staring with growing disapproval. Unreasonable anger was evil, and Gibbie had not often seen it. Now he was seeing it in a minister. Middling good people are shocked at the wickedness of the wicked. Gibbie, who knew both so well, and what ought to be expected, was shocked only at the wickedness of the righteous. Finally the minister realized that his tirade was not working on Gibbie at all. He told Donal to go to bed and Gibbie to get his cap and walk home with him.

Gibbie wrote on a little ivory tablet that Mrs. Sclater had given him for his pocket, "Dear sir, I am going to slepe this night with Donal. The bed is big enuff for 2. Good night, sir."

The boys were courteous as Mr. Sclater left, but Gibbie hurried after him and sneaked all the way home behind him. Donal was alarmed when Gibbie dashed out with no explanation, so he followed Gibbie through the night city and never quite caught up. As Mr. Sclater entered his front door he saw Gibbie behind him and ordered him to come in, but Gibbie lifted his cap in respect and walked on down the street. Donal stayed hidden until Mr. Sclater went inside, and by then

Gibbie had turned a corner. Donal ran and ran, but he finally realized he had lost Gibbie and the Sclater house as well.

Donal didn't even know the name of the street where his new home was. There he was in the middle of the night in a large city, utterly lost, and he never visited more than a tiny country village before. He wandered for miles in the dreary darkness. Finally he passed a tall woman under a street lamp.

"Man," she said, "I've set eyes on your face before! Where do you come from?"

"That's what I'd like to know," Donal said truthfully. "I've seen your eyes before, but I can't see your face."

"Do you know a place called the Mains of Glashruach?" As she asked, she let her shawl open from her face like two curtains.

"Lord! It's the tramp!" cried Donal. "No offense, Ma'am. We thought you drowned when you sailed away on the raft."

"I wouldn't do such a mad thing again to save my life," she answered with a short laugh. "But the Almighty carried me through. And how's little Sir Gibbie? Come in. I don't know your name, but we're just at the door of my place. Come quiet up the stair and tell me."

Donal was very tired and glad to have company. He followed her up to her small room and thought it was nice although his mother would have thought it far from tidy. Donal declined the glass of whisky the woman poured for him, so after a while she sipped it herself. She told him a great deal about Gibbie and his father and promised to tell him someday about her trip on the raft. It wasn't funny at the time, but it was very funny to remember.

When she found out that Donal didn't know where his new home was, she got him to describe it and she knew the place. She took him there right away.

Mistress Croale had not gone downhill since Sambo's murder. It had shocked her into realizing how she had lost her respectability. As a peddler she walked a lot in the open air carrying a heavy basket, and this was good for her health. She was less of a ruin after her years of wandering than at the beginning.

When she received her hundred pounds for finding Sir Gibbie she rented a little shop at the market to sell her wares. Now she did not consume in three days so much whisky as she used to consume in one day. Her face was a little clearer, her eyes were less fierce, and some of the other shopkeepers had grown a little friendly. More important, the poor women who bought things from her had learned to trust her. She was a kind and helpful shopkeeper. There are so many who are sober for one who is honest! She made a living, did not go into debt, spent much of her profits on drink, and had a small measure of respectability again. Still she didn't want to face Gibbie or Mistress Murkison, Donal's landlady, who had known her in her better days.

Mistress Murkison was delighted when she found Donal at the door. Gibbie had come and gone out again looking for him.

"There would be small good in my going to look for him," Donal remarked to her. "It would be the sheep going to look for the shepherd."

When Gibbie came back again Donal let him in. They laughed over the whole affair and went to bed.

43

THE MINISTER'S DEFEAT

MR. SCLATER SMOLDERED WITH ANGER all night and was gloomy at breakfast. He wouldn't admit to his wife that anything was wrong, because he thought he had to seem dignified to her. He didn't know yet if a man is true his friends and loved ones will take care of his dignity for him. He was used to respect from his wife and obedience from his church workers, and so it seemed odd that rude behavior from an ignorant country dummy could upset him so. But he kept puzzling about why Gibbie had followed him home unless it was as a deliberate insult. And if he had no power over Gibbie now, how would it be in the future? If he got power over Gibbie and made Gibbie hate him, then as soon as Gibbie turned twenty-one he would be a liberated enemy who would go straight to the dogs and take his fortune with him! It was all very annoying.

Gibbie entered Mr. Sclater's study at ten o'clock for his lesson as usual, smiling and nodding politely. He sat down with his slate and book ready.

Mr. Sclater said sternly, "Sir Gilbert, what was your meaning in following me home last night?"

Gibbie's face flushed. Mr. Sclater took that as a sign that he was ashamed and got ready to overwhelm him with correction and discipline. Gibbie quickly wrote on his slate and handed it over.

"I thougt you was drunnk."

Mr. Sclater shot up, his face white and eyes flaming. He brought the slate down so hard on Gibbie's head that it flew apart in pieces. Gibbie was stunned. He jumped up like an angry animal, then instantly smiled to show his affection. But Mr. Sclater was stumbling backward over a small stool and landed awkwardly on his back.

Gibbie rushed to help, and Mr. Sclater struck at him in self-defense. Gibbie clamped his arms to the floor, kissed him on the forehead, and helped him up like a child. On his feet again, Mr. Sclater was horrified at what he had done. Gibbie's forehead had blood on it. Mrs. Sclater and Donal were nearby in the drawing-room, and Gibbie might show it to them.

"I'm sorry," he said, "but how dare you write such an insult to me?"

Gibbie wrote on a small piece of broken slate, "I thout it was always whisky that made people act like that. I begg your parden. I will kno better next time, sir."

Gibbie washed his forehead and they did the lessons that day on paper instead of slate. Gibbie didn't get close to Mrs. Sclater in bright light for a few days so she wouldn't see his small wound and ask about it. From that day on Gibbie came and went as he pleased after lunch. Mrs. Sclater asked him to let them know if he would be with Donal after ten o'clock at night and he never failed once. He was completely dependable and caused them no worry.

That very evening they had friends to dinner. Gibbie's manners were already so good that he could have eaten anywhere without attracting attention. But at this meal he attracted much attention because he kept springing up to serve people. Finally Mrs. Sclater tactfully asked him not to wait on people when servants were in the room because it confused them to have an extra helper. She was so kind that Gibbie thought she gave him permission to serve whenever the servants left the room, and he continued to serve quietly and gracefully.

160

After dessert the ladies left the room and a servant set on the table things for the men to use to make hot toddy. Gibbie had not seen these things since he had fled the city, and they brought back horrible memories of his father and Sambo. A shadow fell upon his soul.

"The girl forgot the whisky," the minister exclaimed. "Sir Gilbert, would you be so good as to bring me the bottle from the shelf?"

Gibbie was frozen, his smile gone.

"It's just behind you, that purple bottle with the silver top."

Tears were running down Gibbie's face.

"I beg your pardon, Sir Gilbert," the minister said as he got the bottle for himself. "I thought you liked serving. Sit down and have a little toddy with us."

Gibbie burst into sobs and darted out to go to his room. He felt terrible about not obeying Mr. Sclater's request and terrible about having been asked to help people to make toddy in the minister's house. It seemed far worse to him there than in Mistress Croale's house by the river. The guests stared, bewildered. Mr. Sclater smoothed it over by telling the odd boy's history so far as he knew it.

The next morning Mrs. Sclater talked with Gibbie about why he must not do what servants are paid to do now that he was a gentleman. Gibbie thought she wanted to know why he had done it. He brought her a New Testament and pointed to the words of Jesus, "I am among you as he that serveth." As soon as she read it he pointed to "The disciple is not above his master, but every one that is perfect shall be as his master."

She was shocked that he dared to try to live out such sacred words in real life. It was preposterous and uncomfortable. But Gibbie didn't do it by serving at her dinner table again.

44

MISTRESS CROALE'S VISIT

MR. SCLATER TOOK GIBBIE to a highly respected doctor right away to see if Gibbie could ever speak. The doctor dashed all his hopes, but Gibbie was not at all disappointed. Sight and hearing were precious to him, not speech. He loved everyone else's voice, not his own. As soon as Mrs. Sclater knew that Gibbie's handicap was permanent she began to learn sign language and to teach it to Gibbie.

If Gibbie had been able to talk, she thought, he would not seem quite so much a gentleman. He would have always been saying the right thing in the wrong place. By "the wrong place" she meant the place where his words would be very meaningful. A certain disappointment followed her first rapid success with his manners. They retained a certain simplicity she called childishness, but it was really childlikeness. Gibbie was incapable of putting on "company manners" of any sort. He was the same for anyone.

Mistress Croale finally decided to try to see Gibbie, who was almost her only pleasant memory. She dressed a little better than usual for work one day and set out for the Sclater home after she had closed her little box of a shop in the evening. It was cold and frosty, and she got chilled waiting at the front door as the maid went to tell her master that there was a poor woman at the door wanting to see Sir Gilbert.

The Sclaters were in the middle of the first course of their dinner, nice hot cockie-leekie soup. The cock is the chicken and the leek is the onion in that tasty dish. Gibbie put down his spoon and was going to the door to see who was waiting for him, but Mr. Sclater stopped him.

"Tell her we're at dinner and she may return in an hour," Mr. Sclater said to the maid. "No. Tell her to come back tomorrow morning."

But Gibbie had already darted out and was bringing Mistress Croale in. She had no idea that he was steering her to the dining room, and she flushed and drew back a step when she saw that she was intruding upon a meal. But the bright fireplace, the rich crimson wallpaper, and the delicious odor of the soup made her think that she could give up whisky more easily if she had the comfortable life of the minister. Gibbie kept trying to pull her to the table.

"Gilbert," Mrs. Sclater whispered loudly, "if you are to be a gentleman and live in my house you must behave yourself. I cannot have a woman like that sitting at my table." Meanwhile, the minister was ushering Mistress Croale out as fast as he could.

"Sir Gilbert!" he exclaimed angrily, "go back to your dinner immediately! Jane, open the door."

The maid opened the door and Mistress Croale stepped out. But there she told the minister that it was no wonder her kind didn't go to church to hear the gospel preached, since they didn't see it practiced by the preacher. If he had offered her a bowl of hot cockie-leekie she would have gone home and read her Bible and then attended church on Sunday. But this way she would go home and drink whisky and the sin of it, if it is a sin to drink whisky in such cold weather, would be his, not hers.

"You are more than welcome to a bowl of soup!" he said dramatically. "Jane, take Mistress Croale into the kitchen to eat, and—"

"The devil's tail in your soup!" Mistress Croale cried. "Since when am I a beggar? It was courtesy I wanted, not soup!" With that she left.

"Really, Sir Gilbert," the minister complained; but Gibbie was gone. He had rushed off after his old friend to spend the evening with her.

"The devil's tail in your soup!" Mistress Croale cried.
"Since when am I a beggar? It was courtesy I wanted, not soup!"

"That's his New Testament again!" Mrs. Sclater exclaimed. The truth is that she was jealous that Gibbie had left her and his nice hot dinner to go off with the poor sinful woman. After a while she added, "You must teach him the absurdity of trying to live according to words that were fine when they were spoken but that are impossible to take literally nowadays." After dinner Mr. and Mrs. Sclater attended a missionary meeting. They decided not to mention Gibbie's latest misbehavior to him.

45

BACK AT THE BAKERY

GIBBIE GOT THE HABIT OF VISITING DONAL every Friday afternoon and staying until Saturday afternoon. One bright cold day when snow was on the ground Mrs. Sclater decided to check on the boys. She looked merry with her fur muff, rosy cheeks, and shining eyes. As she walked toward Donal's place she glanced into a bakery shop and saw Gibbie inside.

He was perched on the counter eating a penny loaf. That irritated her because she knew he had finished a good lunch before he left home. Then she saw that Gibbie was enjoying a visit with a very pretty girl behind the counter. She was much upset.

The girl was Missie, and the two were laughing about the lost earring Gibbie had found for her once and other events of their childhood. Mrs. Sclater walked in quickly and said, "I thought you had gone to see Donal!" Gibbie explained that Donal was going to meet him in the bakery shop to go for a walk on the pier, and that he and Missie were old friends. Then Missie told Mrs. Sclater a bit about poor little Gibbie of the old days. Missie was charming and Gibbie was delighted with her memories, but Mrs. Sclater was more annoyed than interested. She wanted Gibbie's past forgotten.

When Donal and Gibbie left, she stayed and said a few words to Missie alone that hurt the girl's feelings and caused her to avoid

Gibbie for a long time. Mrs. Sclater meant well, but she was all wrong. Gibbie was in no danger of marrying the bakery girl.

Mrs. Sclater had pretended she didn't understand that Gibbie wanted to visit Miss Kimble's school, but needed help to find it. When he had seen Miss Kimble's schoolgirls at church Mrs. Sclater would always slow him down so he didn't get close to them. But now that Mrs. Sclater thought Gibbie was in love with a baker's daughter, she decided that Gibbie should meet some refined girls from Miss Kimble's school after all.

One day at lunch Mrs. Sclater told Gibbie that he should dress up because some ladies were coming to tea. So it was that Gibbie and Ginevra found themselves shaking hands in Mrs. Sclater's drawing-room. Then Gibbie rushed off without any explanation to get Donal to share in the pleasure.

Donal was studying hard when Gibbie came in. When he learned that Ginevra was visiting Gibbie he forgot about studying and everything else. His mind was like a whirlwind. Shy as he was about city manners, he would risk anything to see the lovely lady-girl. It took Donal a long time to get washed and dressed up to go to tea at the Sclater house. He couldn't have chosen worse looking clothes to wear; they were cheap and flashy. But neither Donal nor Gibbie noticed that he was dressed in poor taste. By the time they got to the Sclater house refreshments were all over and both Mr. and Mrs. Sclater were talking to the guests, wondering where Gibbie was.

46

DONAL IN SOCIETY

WHEN THE MAID OPENED THE DOOR, Donal spent a full minute wiping his shoes on the mat, as if he were walking in from a farmyard. Gibbie led him in triumph to the drawing room. There Donal went right across the room to Ginevra and took the hand she timidly held out to him, shaking it gently and holding it a long time. Gibbie danced about behind him in joy. When Ginevra sat down and Donal looked around for a chair, he saw Mrs. Sclater and walked across to her in his rolling, loose-jointed stride.

"How are you this afternoon, Ma'am? I didn't see your lovely face when I came in. A grand house like this—it's none too grand to fit you, I'm sure—but it is a bit confusing to plain folk like me, used to being out in the open meadows with Gibbie."

"A natural gentleman," she thought. "I could teach him quickly."

Aloud she said, "You will soon get acquainted with city ways, Mr. Grant. Would you oblige me by calling Gilbert by his own name—*Sir* Gilbert, please? I don't care, but I wish him to get used to it or I wouldn't ask." She put him at ease with a squeeze of his hand and had him sit near Ginevra.

To Miss Kimble and the two girls who had come with Ginevra, Donal looked very odd. As he talked to Ginevra in his old-fashioned country style, they thought he sounded odd. He told Ginevra about a dream he had in which he turned into an ugly enchanted snake looped around a tree three times, like that in the ballad of *Kemp Owen* he had once read to her. In his dream a lady-knight came in armor and he hoped that she would break the spell. When he tried to ask her for help, all he could do was to hiss at her. She looked at him a long time and could not decide to kiss him to break the spell, and finally she sighed and sadly left him with no hope.

Ginevra had been listening intently, and at the end tears spilled from her eyes. The other girls had listened closely also, looking at Donal as if they saw a peacock's feather in a turkey tail because he was such a good story teller. But no one understood at the time that the lady-knight in the dream was Ginevra. Only Donal knew that.

Next Gibbie began to teach Ginevra the finger alphabet, and the other girls watched with great interest. Then Mrs. Sclater played the piano and sang. She invited Miss Kimble to play; but Miss Kimble was not musical, and so she asked Ginevra to sing her song. Only the three from Glashgar knew that the song Ginevra sang had been written by Donal. That made his visit complete.

After that, everyone went to the dining-room for supper, and Donal slipped out instead because he knew he was not invited. He ran home to the furniture shop and his books, ready to study again.

Gibbie walked back to the school with his visitors after supper. Now he knew where Ginevra lived. But when he went to visit her at the school she had to tell him that Miss Kimble didn't want him coming there.

47

A HUMBUG IN THE PULPIT

MR. SCLATER FOLLOWED HIS WIFE'S REQUEST and lectured Gibbie that it is a mistake to try to follow the teachings of Jesus. Some of the points he made were partially right, but through his whole lecture there was no hint of enthusiasm about the gospel, no hint that Christ was his refuge or his delight. It seemed as if God was the soap and water with which he blew word bubbles when he preached, and no more. Gibbie listened politely, but he wasn't convinced.

Gibbie believed that Jesus meant it when he said, "If you love me, keep my commandments." After Mr. Sclater finished, Gibbie remembered who had talked like that before. It was Mr. Worldly Wiseman in *Pilgrim's Progress*. He had read Janet's copy several times at Glashgar. Now he asked Mrs. Sclater if he could look at her copy. She peeked to see what part he was reading, and when she saw that it was the part about Mr. Worldly Wiseman, she knew that Gibbie was comparing him to her husband. She told Mr. Sclater, and he was embarrassed that his wife would guess what Gibbie had in mind. They both expected Gibbie to point out Mr. Worldly Wiseman to them, but he was learning to be more tactful than that. They were simply not the disciples of the Carpenter that he had expected them to be.

The next Sunday in church, Mr. Sclater saw from the pulpit that a poor old man had come in the side door that was near the pew where

Gibbie and Mrs. Sclater always sat. No usher helped the man. Gibbie quietly went to get him and caused him to sit down next to Mrs. Sclater with her satin cape and sable muff. She moved as far as she could from him—flushed, angry, uncomfortable. The disgust in her eyes upset her husband and caused him to get his words confused in the opening prayer. He agreed with her, and yet for the first time in his life he wondered if he was a bit of a humbug. Gibbie and the poor old man sat through the service in peaceful satisfaction, understanding nothing at all of the sermon.

The Sclaters didn't scold Gibbie. Instead they protected themselves from him in three ways. They spoke to the usher about guarding Mrs. Sclater from riffraff. She began to make Gibbie enter the pew first so he couldn't get out easily. And they removed their New Testament from the drawing-room so he couldn't show them verses in it any more.

48

DONAL'S HEART AND MIND

DONAL HAD TO ATTEND MR. SCLATER'S CHURCH because the minister insisted upon it when he brought him to the city. Donal enjoyed seeing Gibbie and Ginevra at a distance at church, but he found the sermons a trial. Many of Mr. Sclater's sermons were long arguments against errors that no one in his congregation had ever heard of, and that is part of the reason that Gibbie could not make head nor tail of them. Donal wrote funny verses about Mr. Sclater and his useless sermons, but he never showed them to Gibbie because he knew that Gibbie was fond of his guardian.

Mrs. Sclater asked Gibbie to urge Donal to improve his clothing and his style of speech so people wouldn't think he was ridiculous. The wisest and best of men are ignored, she explained, if they don't look and speak like other people. Gibbie thought to himself that her rule didn't apply to John the Baptist. He explained that Donal could speak fine English, but that he chose to use his old country Scottish instead in order to be loyal to his background. He didn't want to put on airs like Fergus Duff. Donal's clothes simply reflected the fact that he was poor.

Mr. Sclater advised Gibbie to buy new clothes for Donal, acting as if money he could provide for the purpose was more his than Gibbie's. But Donal refused Gibbie's gift and wore only clothes that he could afford. Eventually he saw how bad his best suit looked on him, but he continued to wear it until it wore out although it embarrassed him. He did allow Mrs. Sclater to convince him that it is courteous to speak like the people you are with instead of continuing to talk like the people you used to be with. He soon spoke better English than Mr. Sclater. But he still spoke his old way with Gibbie and when he prayed to God.

"How will you speak when you are a minister?" Gibbie asked with his fingers.

"Me, a minister?" Donal exclaimed. He went on to tell Gibbie that he hoped to be a schoolteacher. Otherwise he would be a shepherd like his father. He would have to enlarge his parents' cottage if he lived there so he would have room for all his books. He would always want lots of books and time to read. He wouldn't get newspapers often because they are largely a waste of time. They tell things before they are sure, so you have to read out of your mind one day what you read into it the day before. You might as well wait until matters are more settled.

Gibbie asked Donal about his hopes for a wife and children.

"No wife for me, Gibbie! Who would want a poor schoolteacher or a shepherd? Only some girl like my sister who doesn't love poetry and education." Donal was, in his way, in love with Ginevra. But he didn't dream of marrying her.

Gibbie showed Donal many places from his childhood including the Old House of Galbraith. Sir George's shed for cobbling had been taken away piece by piece and used for firewood. The garret was just as they had left it. No one lived there because it was said to be haunted. People believed that every Sunday Sir George could be heard pounding on shoes for his little boy until dark. Then he cried out to God for mercy. Poor people didn't even like to live in other parts of the building any more because of the haunting.

"If I were you," Donal advised, "I would tell Mr. Sclater to watch for his first chance to buy this house for you. It would be a shame if you didn't get to own your family home."

"How can I?" Gibbie asked. "The money isn't mine yet."

"Yes, it is yours now!" Donal answered. "You can't lay your hands on it yet. The sooner you let Mr. Sclater know that you know what you're doing, the better. He'll get you this house."

Donal was right. Mr. Sclater soon bought the house for Gibbie, never knowing that Donal had advised Gibbie to ask for it.

Donal went on living above the furniture store. Sometimes when the moon was shifting into the storage area outside his room Donal would open his door and gaze into the dim confusion as if looking into a faded dream. Then sometimes he would walk up and down among the spider-legged tables, tall cabinets, and secret-looking bureaus, imagining all kinds of sad, romantic, or frightening stories. Donal was the kind who needed no drugs to set him dreaming and to make his life intensely exciting. He was also the kind who needed no books to set him thinking and creating. When he returned to farm work during his very long summer vacations he kept on growing wiser and making verses all the time.

Gibbie got to spend six wonderful weeks of every summer at home with Robert and Janet while the Sclaters went on vacation. It was just like before except that Gibbie had more things to think about now and more ways of thinking about them. Once he and Donal carried wood and mortar up the mountain so that Gibbie could build a little enclosed porch on the cottage to keep the wind away from the door. There was hardly anything else his aging parents wanted in this world.

49

THE BEGGAR

WHEN DONAL'S LAST WINTER in college began, Gibbie was ready to start college. Mr. Sclater had him compete for a scholarship, and he won a good one and then refused to take it. Scholarships are meant to help boys like Donal, he explained, not rich boys who don't need them.

Mr. Sclater had realized soon after he began to teach Gibbie that he was an excellent student. He became an excellent writer. Gibbie paid no attention to the way other people wrote in order to seem elegant. All he cared about was to say what he meant and to avoid saying something else; to know when he had not said what he meant, and to set the words right. His writing was clear and direct and could hardly ever be improved.

The college was too far from the Sclater home, and so Gibbie decided to live with Donal. Mr. Sclater wanted them to move to a better neighborhood, away from the furniture shop. But Gibbie wanted to be loyal to the kind Mistress Murkison, and he rented a room from her. The Sclaters let Gibbie have his way with no argument because they understood him better as time passed and they understood better what was good. He had changed them slowly for the better by living with them.

One night the boys had taken a long walk and come home late. Near their home they met a ghostly woman in rags, with a white, worn face, and the largest black eyes they had ever seen. She carried a puny baby wrapped tight in the corner of her black shawl. Her eyes were wild with trouble. She hesitated, half stopped, and held out a white hand.

Donal had no money, but Gibbie had a shilling. She took it with a gleam, murmured some thanks, and walked on. They were so concerned about her wandering alone in the cold night fog that they followed her at a great distance. At last they peered into a dirty little shop she had entered and watched her drink a shilling's worth of whisky from a broken teacup. To the horror of the boys, she put some of it into her baby's mouth from her own. Then she came out, and Donal lost his self-control.

"Hey," he cried, "that wasn't what you got the shilling for!"

"You didn't say anything," she answered softly as she walked on with her head down, squeezing her baby to her.

"It isn't right to give shillings to people like that," Donal said to Gibbie. "It probably does more harm than good."

He stopped because Gibbie was weeping. He wanted to save the woman and her baby. Love seemed hopeless, for money was useless.

That hour his heart began to be haunted by the homeless and hungry. It was a good haunting that would lead to good action. To the true heart every doubt is a door.

The boys followed the woman to an even worse part of the city, where she finally went into a dreadful building for the night. Relieved that she was not out in the cold, the boys went home. In the morning their first words were about the woman.

"If only my mother were here to help us," Donal said.

"Shall we ask Mr. Sclater's advice?" Gibbie suggested.

Donal laughed. "He would tell her to feel ashamed of herself, and I think she has done that long ago. He would tell her to get a job and earn a decent living, and she probably can't do anything worth a dollar a day."

It ended in their going to Mistress Croale, asking her to find out who the woman was and what could be done for her. She was happy that the boys wanted her help; it gave her a feeling of dignity. Finding out something about the poor drunken woman for a good cause did Mistress Croale herself much good.

The boys had another strange meeting at that time. They were near the gate of Miss Kimble's school, and out came a thin, care-worn man in shabby clothes. His shoulders were hunched forward as if an invisible thing had jumped upon him from behind. He often straightened up and tried to walk erect. It was Mr. Galbraith. The boys lifted their caps in respect, but he didn't seem to notice them.

50
FERGUS'S STYLE

MR. GALBRAITH WAS a thoroughly ruined man. He took Ginevra out
of her school and they moved into a very small house that belonged
to her from her mother. The little house had a tiny flower garden in
front, and as soon as he moved in he had the railing lined with boards
so that people going by would not be able to look at the flowers any
more. He could not bear to live without the dignity of being the lord
of Glashruach and chairman of a great company. When Mr. and Mrs.
Sclater came to visit him, he pretended that he wasn't home. He
couldn't face people.

Nothing interested him any more. His eyes were more unsteady, his
lips looser, his neck thinner and longer, and his body like a puppet
with loose strings. He would sit for hours without moving. It was sad
to Ginevra to see her father withered and idle, and she spent much
time sitting silently near him when she would have preferred reading.
He insisted to himself that she was heartless and cold because she was
calm and peaceful. Whenever she tried to signal some kind of caring
or cheer or sympathy to him, he responded by acting as blind and
stiff as a corpse.

One brilliant frosty morning Mrs. Sclater rang the bell on the gate.
Ginevra found that the lady and Gibbie had come to take her for a
walk. She went and asked her father for permission, not mentioning
that Gibbie had come along.

"Why do you ask me?" he sulked. "You have never paid any attention to my wishes."

She offered to stay home with him if he wished it.

"By no means. If you stay home I'll go out alone and dine at the Red Hart." He named the most expensive restaurant he could think of, knowing he didn't have enough money to pay for a meal there.

This made Ginevra miserable, but she put on her brown-ribboned bonnet and got out the moth-eaten muff that had been her mother's. Life in her was strong, and with her friends she soon forgot her father's mean spirit.

Donal was waiting on the corner, looking warm and healthy without an overcoat. He was wearing new clothes that were appropriate and that fit him, and he greeted Ginevra with real charm. Soon he had made her cheerful as they walked along. They crossed the bridge over the Daur River where Gibbie had crossed after Sambo's death, and he told them all the story for the first time, using his fingers and gestures.

Close to the city there was a rock-bordered cliff above the sea, and there they walked until they came across the Reverend Duff by accident.

"I have not had the pleasure of seeing you since you were a little girl, Miss Galbraith," said Fergus.

Ginevra told him coolly that she didn't remember him. Gibbie and Donal were used to seeing him at times at college and greeted him in a relaxed way.

When they met him, Fergus had been practicing a sermon he was to deliver at a big city church the next day. He would preach there several Sundays, and he was hoping to be hired there because that church needed a minister.

"I was watching these waves when you found me; they seem to me such a picture of the vanity of human endeavor! But just as these waves would not heed me if I told them they were wasting their labor on these rocks, so men will not heed me tomorrow when I tell them of the emptiness of their ambitions." Fergus was acting the part of a clergyman for the ladies.

Donal pointed out that Fergus was himself an example of a waste of effort if he knew the people weren't going to hear what he tried to say to them and he said it anyway. Fergus ignored him.

"Just as these waves waste themselves in an effort to tear down the rocks, so do worldly men go on spending their strength for nothing."

"Fergus!" Donal interrupted. "Do you think the waves don't know their business better than to think they have to tear down these rocks?"

Fergus looked at Donal with scorn. This was only a cowherd. "I spoke poetically," he said with cold dignity. "I personified the waves."

"The very heart of poetry is truth," Donal answered, "and so what you said is not poetic. There is true and false personification, and a false one is no more to me than a duck quack. If a very good poet doesn't watch out he might blather nonsense about the sea warring against the rocks and such stuff. It's to be avoided."

"But the waves really do wear down the rocks by slow degrees," Fergus retorted.

"Then they aren't wasting their labor after all and where is your sermon?" Donal answered. He went on a great deal more about the harmony and unity of nature, the design at the heart of creation, and truth in poetry.

"I hope, ladies, that this flood of philosophy didn't make you feel dizzy," Fergus said with a smile of superiority curling his lip. "I can't understand such ideas, especially in old-fashioned country language. Can you?"

"Perfectly," said Mrs. Sclater. "You have a poor opinion of our brains." She found Donal far more impressive than Fergus.

Fergus decided to leave out the part of his sermon about waves ruining themselves on the rocks they hoped to destroy. He would add something about winter winds and snow instead. He got Ginevra's address from her in hopes of visiting her father; and then he left, nursing his dignity.

On Monday, Fergus went to visit Mr. Galbraith and was pleased to visit Ginevra instead because her father refused to come out of his room. Ginevra did not enjoy Fergus, and if she had seen him preach she would have liked him even less. He used long words, waved his arm, threw forward his hands, raised his voice, and wiped his eyes with a large, fancy handkerchief.

The second time that Fergus came to the house Mr. Galbraith came out to see what he wanted. Fergus was so flattering that the old man felt every inch a lord again and invited him to return.

Remembering that the lord liked to play backgammon, Fergus asked for a game. From then on he spent at least one evening a week trying to draw Mr. Galbraith out of his gloom. His reason was that he was charmed by Ginevra and wanted to marry her.

51
FERGUS'S GLORY

IT WAS AN ICE-COLD SUNDAY NIGHT in March, cloudy and blowing. The wind felt black, the sky was black, and the streetlamps were bobbing as if trying to escape the darkness instead of fighting it. The large North Church was packed early with eager people who had come to hear the preaching of the new minister who had just been appointed. They filled the pews, stood in the aisles, and even perched on the window sills. They were waiting to watch some fireworks of words; the preacher was about to flash sparklers of logic and eloquence over the dark canyon of truth and toss a few firecracker ideas into the void.

Donal and Gibbie searched the crowd and saw the back of Ginevra's brown bonnet near the front of the church. Donal had already heard that Fergus Duff visited the Galbraiths often, and it was unendurable to him to think of Ginevra marrying such a windbag. He realized that Thomas Galbraith would resent marrying his daughter to the son of John Duff, who had rented farmland from him, but that John Duff's modest wealth and Fergus Duff's good income were enough to overcome the impoverished man's pride.

Donal had no idea how Ginevra liked the sermon. He now realized that he had always talked so much when he was with her that he knew very little of how she thought. Most of the congregation listened spellbound, but Donal listened with absolute scorn. Gibbie disliked the sermon also, preferring the dull ones of Mr. Sclater that didn't say anything. Fergus gave a glowing description of the gold and jewels in the city of God, but said nothing about why a Christian would want to go to such a place. He gave an excited description of hell, but no hint of the real reason it would be tragic to go there—being separated from the love of God.

At last he and his flowing black robe sank exhausted into his chair and it was over. Donal and Gibbie hurried outside and around to wait at the door where Ginevra and her father should come out. The clouds had parted, and a glorious full moon was shining. Ginevra and her father came out, already joined by Fergus Duff.

"Oh, Mr. Duff!" Mr. Galbraith said. "Would you start walking home with my daughter? I'll catch up soon. I have to see a friend."

Donal and Gibbie watched long enough to see that this was a lie. He had no one there. Then they hurried after Fergus and Ginevra, overtaking them at her gate. The four greeted each other politely.

"Such a grand night!" Donal said. "The moon looks bright enough to keep the clouds away from her, doesn't she? But there's a big black one with a little white collar that I think is going to overcome her soon. He'll take her in his arms and blot out all her light. Good night, miss. Good night, Fergus. You ministers shouldn't dress yourselves so much like clouds, Fergus. You should dress bright like the New Jerusalem you tell such tales about."

Donal walked away with Gibbie, and then he soon broke down.

"Gibbie," he said, "that rascal's going to marry Ginevra! It drives me mad. If I could just once speak to her!"

Gibbie's face grew white in the moonlight and his lips trembled. When they got home Donal was so sad that he closed himself in his room. It was still early, so Gibbie hurried off to have a talk with Mrs. Sclater. She understood, and invited the two friends to visit her Monday evening.

52
DONAL'S DEFEAT

IT WAS MONDAY OF DONAL'S final week in college. To him grades and graduation seemed unimportant now. He and Gibbie walked through night air so cold that it felt like the sharp edge of an axe of cold that cuts to the soul. Then they entered Mrs. Sclater's crimson-walled dining room with its large round table set for a hearty Scotch tea. The blazing fireplace welcomed them, and by it sat Ginevra! Mrs. Sclater kept the fire going and kept the conversation going.

After the meal Gibbie asked Ginevra if she would like to go for a walk. Mrs. Sclater graciously approved of Ginevra taking a stroll with Gibbie and Donal although, to tell the truth, it was not quite proper for a girl of her class to go out for a walk at night with young men.

Donal and Ginevra walked close and spoke softly while Gibbie flitted to and fro around them. Donal asked her how she had liked Fergus's sermon.

"Papa thought it was grand," she said. "He tells me I am no judge."

"So you didn't like it as well as he did!"

"I kept wondering what your mother would say about this or that. For you know, any good there is in me I have gotten from her, and from Gibbie—and from you, Donal." After a while she added, "How did you like the sermon? Do you think it might frighten some into repentance?"

Donal's heart had been beating hard with pleasure. Trying not to be harsh with Fergus, he answered, "Maybe so; I don't know. But it's a pagan kind of repentance that can't do much good in the long run, in my opinion, because it left out God. I can't think much of a sermon that gets people to think more of the preacher than of him that he came to preach about. I don't see how anyone could love God or his neighbor a bit more for having heard it."

"I felt that way," Ginevra answered. "I'm sorry if Mr. Duff has to teach things he doesn't understand."

Soon they were out of the city, and Donal invited Ginevra to put her hand on his arm as they walked. He trembled at her touch. He made up a few joyful lines of poetry for her and she begged him to repeat them, but he said he couldn't recall them because she was all he could think about.

At that point she wanted to change the subject. She asked him what lay off the road, and he told her it was the great stone quarry. Stone from it had built most of the city. He offered to show it to her if she wasn't afraid to see it by moonlight.

"No, Donal. I would not be frightened to go anywhere with you."

Gibbie waited on the road, thinking they would take a look and come right back. When they did not return he followed them.

In his eagerness Donal led Ginevra farther and farther, all the way to the bottom of the strange quarry pit. It reminded her of a nightmare she had once. When he thought she was wanting to turn back, he sang her the first song that came into his head. It happened to be a depressing song about death, coffin lids, worms, and forsaken love. She thought it was dreadful, but did not say so. The dark rocky pit was a place of terror to her. She was trying to be brave and trust him.

At the bottom Donal suddenly caught her hand and called her by her first name. He had never done that before. He said that she was a grand lady and he was only a shepherd. She answered that he was a great poet.

Then Donal poured out his heart to Ginevra. He said he would finish college now and go away to work as a shepherd, never to see her again. He told her that he would gladly cut his head off and place it under her feet to keep them off the cold floor. He tried to tell her how pretty she was and how she filled his mind and heart. He wanted to beg something from her that would make a difference to him the rest of his life.

"What is it, Donal?" she whispered. She could barely say anything.

He went on talking as if she hadn't spoken, finally telling her what he begged for—that she would kiss him just once. It would be holy to him as the light, he said, a favor from her sweet soul to him. No one on earth, not even Gibbie, would ever know. That made Ginevra interrupt him. "But, Donal," she said quietly, "would that be right? Never to tell *anyone*?"

Donal's face instantly twisted in despair. The look terrified her.

"Gibbie! Gibbie!" she screamed. He was approaching just then and ran to her. She darted to him like a dove pursued by a hawk, threw herself into his arms, and wept.

Finally she sobbed, "I couldn't let Donal think I might have married him if things were different. I couldn't. It's not because he's a shepherd at all. I couldn't, could I Gibbie?" Gibbie had tears on his cheeks too, although he didn't understand her. He went to look for Donal in the rocky shadows, but Donal was hiding.

Donal had heard Ginevra, and he understood. He hid until his friends gave up and left.

Gibbie took Ginevra home and left her, grief-stricken because he believed she had chosen to marry Fergus. Then he stayed up all night looking for Donal and waiting for Donal with hot tea ready, but Donal never came home. The next day Gibbie caught a glimpse of Donal at college and spent hours looking for him in vain. The next day he watched at a corner and saw Donal go in to take his final examination, looking as if he had not slept at all. On the last day Donal appeared in the auditorium to receive his college degree, but he slipped away when Gibbie tried to get to him afterward. When Gibbie got to his room there was a note from Donal saying good-bye. He asked Gibbie to pack his things in his trunk and leave it with their landlady. He had gone home to Janet.

53

A NIGHT SPY

WHEN GIBBIE READ DONAL'S brief good-bye he knew loneliness as never before. He sat down and wrote a letter to Donal there in the room Donal had enjoyed so much, looking through the open door at times into the dusty room of old furniture. He packed Donal's things and all the books they had bought together. Part of his life was over.

Gibbie was not a person to be deeply troubled. He was lonely, and so he went to see Mistress Croale at her shop. She was overjoyed to see him. He learned that Donal had been staying in her room for a few nights without telling her what the trouble was. She invited Gibbie to come for a little supper at nine and tell her about Donal then. He nodded and left her.

All this time Miss Kimble had been standing at the next counter with her face hidden from Gibbie, listening to Mistress Croale. She was a newcomer to the city and knew nothing about Gibbie's background. With self-congratulation that she had proved Gibbie a low character with bad taste, she hurried off to report her discovery to his uncle, Mr. Thomas Galbraith. She felt she had uncovered a scandal.

Fergus was there when she rang the bell. Mr. Galbraith thought she had come to try to collect money he owed her, and he closed himself in his room. So she told her tale to Fergus and Ginevra, identifying Gibbie as Ginevra's cousin.

"I was not aware that Sir Gilbert was a cousin of yours, Miss Galbraith," said Fergus.

Ginevra blushed and said he was certainly not her cousin.

"Why Ginevra! You told me he was your cousin," the confused Miss Kimble cried in anger. "I must see your father instantly!"

Fergus finally rescued everyone by assuring Miss Kimble that he would take care of the matter for her. He walked her home and returned to the Galbraith home for dinner. Then at eight he decided to check on the young man who once served as a brownie. He knew where Mistress Croale lived. He went to her house and watched Gibbie go in at nine.

For two hours Fergus walked around in the cold waiting for Gibbie to come out. He felt it was his duty to be a moral policeman on patrol.

It was hard for Fergus to follow Gibbie once Gibbie did come out, because he was swift as a shadow. Then Gibbie stopped at a poor old woman seated on a doorstep in the cold. After a bit he took her by the hand, and she arose and went with him. She was sober, but she smelled like whisky.

Fergus followed them through several streets and saw them stop at a door. He imagined that the woman gave Gibbie the key to open it. He thought that this was a pretty young woman taking Gibbie into her place for a visit. They went in and Gibbie led her through the furniture storage to his room. There he fed her coffee and bread and butter with marmalade. He turned down the covers on his bed for her and left her alone for a warm night's sleep. He slept in Donal's room. She left early in the morning before Gibbie woke up, stealing one of Mistress Murkison's silver spoons. It was to her credit that of the four in Gibbie's room, she left three. Gibbie bought a whole set of new spoons for Mistress Murkison later.

That same morning Donal mailed a letter to Ginevra. It was delivered the next day to Mr. Galbraith at the breakfast table. He did not receive many letters any more, and so he took this one to his room and read it. It was only sixteen lines of poetry with no explanation, and Mr. Galbraith couldn't understand it. He laid the letter aside and said nothing about it, inwardly angry and contemptuous.

That is why he refused to let Ginevra accept an invitation to spend the evening with Mrs. Sclater. Gibbie was hoping Ginevra would come so he could tell her about Donal. The letter from Donal, which she knew nothing about, only served to increase her isolation.

54
COMING OF AGE

MR. SCLATER DIDN'T KNOW that Donal had urged Gibbie to look up his birthday in the parish registry. Nothing was ever said about it.

"This is my birthday," Gibbie told Mrs. Sclater at breakfast one day in May. Her husband was well aware of the fact, but she didn't know.

"Many happy returns," she said. "How old are you today?"

He held up all his fingers twice, and then one more.

She looked struck and glanced at her husband. He congratulated Gibbie and got up to leave. Then he had to sit back down.

"If you please, sir," Gibbie spelled out, "I want my property now."

"These are not things to be done in a hurry," he answered coolly, as if he had been guardian to twenty wards like Gibbie already. "We'll see in a few days what your lawyer Mr. Torrie thinks. You must learn patience."

"When will you see Mr. Torrie?" Gibbie signaled. Mr. Sclater had already pushed back his plate and cup, a trick to stop conversation, and rose from the table again.

"By and by," he said as he walked toward the door. "It won't hurt you to wait another year or two for the money. You have plenty of time."

"Will you go with me to Mr. Torrie today?"

The minister shook his head no and left. Gibbie seemed disappointed, and Mrs. Sclater told him he didn't understand business. Smiling,

Gibbie got out his writing case and wrote this letter:

> Dear Mr. Sclater,—I am now responsible for my money,
> and if I leave it idle I shall be doing wrong. There are
> things I need to do with it. If you have not gone with me
> to Mr. Torrie by noon, I will go to lawyers Hope & Waver
> instead and find out what to do to get my property. I am
> not a child any longer. I am, dear Mr. Sclater, your affec-
> tionate ward, Gilbert Galbraith.

He left the letter with Mr. Sclater in his study. There was nothing for
Mr. Sclater to do but come out and follow Gibbie's wishes. Mr. Torrie
saw that Gibbie insisted upon understanding everything, so there was
nothing to do but to make it all plain. The three went to a bank,
where Gibbie got a check book.

As they left the bank, Gibbie asked Mr. Sclater if he could stay on at
his house until classes began again in the fall. The minister's change
of tone was startling. He told Gibbie with immense respect that he
hoped he would always consider the Sclater home his own no matter
how many other houses he chose to have.

The first project Gibbie carried through was to restore the Old
House of Galbraith to much of its old magnificence. Thanks to Mr.
Sclater's management, Gibbie owned several other houses in the
neighborhood, and so he was able to move the poor renters out of
the mansion into better places. Then he furnished some of the rooms
with furniture he bought from his old friend Mistress Murkison.
Gibbie did not know yet that Mr. Sclater had also had the foresight to
buy for him secretly the property at Glashruach.

On the day when Gibbie was leaving for his usual summer visit with
Janet, Mr. Sclater finally told him that all of Glashruach was his. Mrs.
Sclater saw Gibbie's eyes and thought fast, then spoke gently.

"How could Mr. Galbraith have taken his wife's property and then
lost it so his daughter didn't get it!"

"I suppose he had bad luck and couldn't help it," Gibbie signalled.

"Bad luck that amounted to swindling," she replied. "He hurt many besides himself. If he had Glashruach once more, he would do it again."

"Then I'll give it to Ginevra," Gibbie responded.

"And let her father take it from her and do harm again!" she said.

Gibbie saw that Mrs. Sclater was right. To give carelessly is not always to bless. He would have to make plans.

When Gibbie got home to the cottage on Glashgar, he learned that Donal had told all his troubles to his mother. She was sad about her son's sorrow, but she said, "Donal will come out of this with more room in his heart and more light in his spirit." She had persuaded him to become a teacher instead of a farm worker, and he had taken a job far away.

Gibbie told Janet that Glashruach was his. Then for the first time she seemed to understand how rich he was. Gibbie offered to make Robert the lord of Glashgar, but Janet asked, "How would Robert be better off if he owned the mountain? No, he's too old for that." Then she advised Gibbie to marry Ginevra and take her back to her own house.

Gibbie gave a great sigh to think of Ginevra shut up in the city, going every Sunday to hear Fergus Duff preach.

The next day he sent for an architect and began working on the ruined house of Glashruach. He put in a huge buttressing wall to make the remains safe. Across the dry stream bed he built a solid stone bridge with a pointed arch, a steep roof, and oriel windows looking up and down the little stream. On the other side he made a new building that featured a high room for Ginevra with a windowed turret sticking out over the stream she loved. Someday Gibbie would make the stream run again. When she was married to Fergus and safe from her father, Gibbie would give this all to her.

His secret was kept perfectly. No one knew who really owned Glashruach.

55

A TRUE WOMAN

ONE COLD AFTERNOON at the end of October, Mistress Croale was about to head home to a cup of hot toddy, but Gibbie came to get her. As she walked with him to her old neighborhood she wondered why she had been haunted by troubles. What would her favorite aunt think of her now? On any night of the week she was apt to go to bed completely drunk. She was afraid she would end up lying dead in her coffin with earth in her mouth, longing for whisky. This had all begun years before when she began to feel it was wrong for her to go on selling whisky, but she had continued anyway. After that she began to drink heavily, and things went wrong.

As they approached the Old House of Galbraith she figured that Gibbie was taking her there to show her where his father had lived in misery and died young because of the whisky she sold him. She figured that Gibbie was going to ask her to stop drinking.

"Well," she said to herself, "I'm a heap better off than I was once, and I'll give it up altogether before I die of it."

Gibbie led her up a dark stairway and opened the door to a grand room with stately furniture. A fire was blazing and candles were lit. The lively table was set for dinner for two.

Gibbie gave her a note that said, "Will you be my housekeeper? I will give you a hundred pounds a year." Her answer was that she would look ridiculous in such a fine setting, silly enough to make the devil laugh.

He took her into a gorgeous bedroom where a hot bath was waiting for her and a rich black satin dress was spread out on the bed. He had got the help of Mrs. Sclater's dressmaker to make ready for her. He left Mistress Croale there to bathe and dress and use the ivory brushes and a great mirror. When she came out she was transformed into a rather handsome woman with tears of gratitude in her eyes. Gibbie danced around her, holding a candle high in admiration. Then they had dinner together.

Afterward he handed her a paper that said, "I agree to work for Sir Gilbert Galbraith. I agree that if I taste whisky once he shall send me away immediately with no warning or discussion." She immediately signed, and they shook hands.

Then he showed her all over the house and explained that he meant to secretly bring homeless people in off the city streets to spend the night there. He would bring them in through a poor little house in back and never let them know where they had been cared for. She had to treat the people as guests and keep his secret. She heartily agreed, remembering her own nights spent outdoors in the cold. He asked her to read Psalm 107 aloud to him from the Bible he had set out. He took away her keys to her tiny shop and her old room and promised to return in a week to live in the Old House with her during his college term.

Mistress Croale looked at herself in a long mirror—one that Donal had often seen himself in. She was almost painfully happy. She had come into warmth and splendor and luxury and bliss! Gibbie had made a lady of her! There was only one thing she needed—a good tumbler of toddy by the fire before she went to bed.

She had some money in her pocket. She could easily go to her old house on Jink Lane, which was still a whisky shop. Who would tell? In a week Sir Gibbie would move in with her and then she would have no more chance. Why not a last good-bye to her old friend Whiskey? Then she imagined Gibbie's face and how sad he would look if she failed him. After all he had done for her!

She locked the door and spent the evening admiring her new things and went to her beautiful bed completely sober. When Gibbie returned a week later he came to a true woman, an honest person who had not cheated.

56

FERGUS'S COURTSHIP

GIBBIE HAD SEEN GINEVRA once that fall at Fergus Duff's church, looking sad and pale. He had gone there just to look for her. He wished he could cause her to marry Donal by giving her Glashruach. He spent several evenings in front of her little house in hopes of seeing her, in vain. He never knocked at the door for fear of displeasing her.

Fergus continued to shower Mr. Galbraith with sincere respect and kindly attention. He had no idea of how the man had ruined himself. The old lord drank twice as much as he had a year ago and tended to tell long, rambling stories; but Fergus stood by him loyally.

When Fergus finally asked permission to court Miss Galbraith, her father exclaimed "The heiress of Glashruach!" and looked at him in scorn. Then he remembered everything and closed his eyes. He thought of all he had to gain with Fergus as his son-in-law. When he opened his unsteady eyes they were rolling like boats on a choppy sea.

"You have my permission, Mr. Duff."

Fergus was not discouraged when Ginevra told him she would not marry him. He was full of confidence. But her father was impatient about her refusal and got out Donal's verses to show Fergus.

"Poetry is nothing but bad prose," he said. "But this may give you a clue about Ginny's refusal. Do you know who wrote this?"

"I think it may be from Donal Grant," Fergus answered. "Or this may be a poem someone copied for her from a newspaper. But whoever wrote the verses, I think that a lady has refused his love."

"That wretch had the impudence to propose to my daughter?" He waved the paper before him and strode into the next room to Ginevra. He didn't pay any attention to the fact that the poem had nothing at all about any marriage proposal and that it didn't mention Ginevra or Donal.

"So you have forgotten all dignity and decency and encouraged a dirty cowherd to propose marriage! It makes my blood boil! You are making me *hate* you!"

Ginevra turned white and asked wisely, "Is that a letter to me that I have not seen?"

"There! Read it! Poetry!"

Tears came to her eyes as she read it and said, "They are only verses saying good-bye."

"What right has that fellow to tell my daughter good-bye? Explain that to me, if you please. For years I knew you liked low company. I hoped you would learn manners as you grew up, although good taste was too much to hope for. You are hankering after that cowherd still or you would not refuse Mr. Duff. This is a disgusting affair, and you are cheap trash!"

He stormed out.

"Her very blood must be tainted," he said to himself, "from her mother's side." From then on he scolded her daily, insisting that the only way for her to make amends for her evil past was to settle down and marry Mr. Duff. She finally gave up trying to defend herself or reason with him and became absolutely silent. He stormed all the more, but she was too depressed to care.

57
GINEVRA'S RESPONSE

MISTRESS CROALE WAS FAST BECOMING an excellent housekeeper. She hoped that some day Gibbie would invite the Sclaters to dinner so she could show them what a skillful and respectable woman she was. She planned to serve them cockie-leekie soup.

Gibbie was a good student and found time to roam the streets for a couple of hours every night looking for guests. Some nights he found none, but other nights he found two or three. He usually sent his guests on their way after breakfast, but sometimes he was able to do more. He saw to it that some of them found jobs. And he kept his identity completely secret.

One midnight Fergus was walking Mr. Galbraith and Ginevra home after a late dinner at his home. He had tried to please Ginevra by including a young lawyer and his wife from the church congregation that evening. The lawyer's wife found Fergus delightful, and he hoped that Ginevra would be influenced by her. As the three walked along they heard coughing and wailing and then saw a sick woman with a child on her lap on a stairway. There was a man soothing a baby near her. Soon they arose and the man carried both children tenderly, leading the woman along as she coughed.

"Look, sir," Fergus exclaimed. "That is the so-called Sir Gilbert Galbraith. They say the foolish boy inherited property. Ginevra knows

They saw a sick woman with a child on her lap on a stairway.
There was a man soothing a baby near her.

200

him slightly, I believe. What will become of him?"

"Good God, Ginny! Do you mean to tell me you have spoken to him? I ask you, and I demand an answer. Why have you concealed from me your acquaintance with this—this—person? There is no such Galbraith. It is a false identity."

"I know him very well," replied Ginevra. "If you really want to know why I did not talk to you about him, it is time for me to tell you what is weighing on my heart."

"Sir Gilbert indeed!" her father muttered in contempt.

Ginevra told her father that when she was a child she had seen Fergus Duff bring a ragged little boy to Glashruach and box his ears on the bridge, an innocent and loving child who had committed no crime except to do good in secret. She had seen her father give him over to Angus MacPholp for a whipping. She had seen the boy fall as if dead.

"Angus gave him merely what he deserved," her father interrupted. "This is cursed folly to cherish resentment all these years against your own father for the sake of a little thieving rascal."

"Please remember," Fergus added humbly, "we didn't know he could not speak."

"You had no heart," she answered. "He ran naked to the mountain and was saved from death by the Grants, who became his parents. Then Angus shot him when he was tending Robert Grant's sheep. Later, Sir Gilbert saved Angus's life in the flood. He saved my life in the flood also, carrying me out of the house just before it fell. But when I told you that, you threw him into a wall and called Angus to whip him again."

"I do remember an insolent fellow intruding into my study."

"And now," Ginevra continued, "Mr. Duff calls him foolish because he is carrying a poor woman's children to get them a bed somewhere!" Then Ginevra burst into tears.

"I always thought she was an idiot!" her father muttered. "Hold your tongue, Ginny! I suppose he told you he was a long-lost cousin of yours? You may have any number of such cousins, if half the stories about your mother's rotten family are true."

Ginevra did not speak another word. When Fergus left them at their door she wouldn't shake hands or say good night.

58
THE LOVE MATCH

GIBBIE HAD SEEN THE THREE watching him as he led the sick mother away, and Ginevra's face told him she needed help. She seemed to say, "Won't you help me although I am not cold and hungry?"

The next day Gibbie hurried home from classes and ate dinner, then set off for Ginevra's little house. At the door he gave the hired girl a card with his name on it for Mr. Galbraith, then followed a bit behind her.

The lord was sitting with Fergus at a small table after dinner. When he read Gibbie's card he cursed, then looked up and saw Gibbie in the middle of the room.

"To what—may I ask—have I—I have not the honor of your acquaintance, Mr.—Mr.—" Here he looked again at the card, put on some glasses, examined the card, and rambled on in a rude way intended to embarrass Gibbie. Then he threw down the glasses and card and glared at Gibbie with his pale, unsteady eyes. It was plain that he had drunk much wine. Gibbie handed him a paper officially promising to give Miss Galbraith all the property of Glashruach on the day of her marriage to Donal Grant.

The lord stretched his neck like a turkey, gobbled, threw the paper at Fergus, glowered at Gibbie, then jumped up and yelled at him.

Fergus, quickly reading the paper for himself, added his voice of protest. "A practical joke! Everybody knows Glashruach is now the property of Major Culsalmon. This is in very bad taste!"

The lord began swearing fiercely at Gibbie, and Fergus turned his attention to him in alarm. "I entreat you to moderate your anger, dear sir." It was useless. The lord was in a mad rage.

"Why don't you speak, you fool?" he thundered. "Go away or, by God, I will break your head! You and your stupid silence!"

Fergus came around the table to get between them, but the lord heaved a heavy pair of nutcrackers at Gibbie's head before Fergus could stop him. The blood spurted out of Gibbie's wound, and he staggered backwards while Fergus seized the lord's arms. Ginevra rushed in and her father broke loose to get at her. He grabbed her roughly and dragged her out of the room.

She resisted and he struck her, causing her to cry for help. By then Fergus was trying to steer Gibbie outside, and at Ginevra's cry Gibbie knocked Fergus down onto the table, shattering wine glasses and china.

Then Gibbie grabbed the lord and swept him into another room, blocking the door. Ginevra was lying on the stairs. He carried her out the door and down some quiet streets.

Ginevra came to her senses, glad to be with Gibbie. They stood and rested under a street light. He explained the message on the paper that had caused all the uproar. He thought it would please her.

"Marry Donal? Oh no," she cried.

"Then be my sister and let me take care of you always. I see that you will never marry anyone."

"Why do you think that?"

"You wouldn't refuse Donal and then marry anyone else, would you?"

Ginevra misunderstood his question in the dim light.

"Yes, Gibbie. I have been yours all the time."

"You would marry me?" he signaled silently. "I never dreamed of such a thing!" He was shocked and confused for the moment.

"Oh no!" she cried. "You don't want me after all! I thought we had an understanding. I thought you were going to marry me some day." She sank to the pavement and sobbed her heart out while he hovered above her and stroked her hand. At last her tears were gone and her sorrow was dry.

"Take me home, Gibbie," she said gently. He helped her up and then she saw his face glorious with joy, like an angel. Rose-fire rushed to her pale cheeks, and she hid her face against his chest. They stood wrapped in each other's arms a long time. She would not have spoken if she could, and he could not have spoken if he would. At last she shivered, and he put his coat on her and buttoned it, laughing. Like two children they hurried along, fearful of pursuit. He brought her to Mrs. Sclater, who heard their story and sent Gibbie away and sent Ginevra to a hot bath and bed.

59

MISTRESS CROALE'S DISASTER

THE MAN WHO LOVES MOST loves best. Gibbie seemed to float along in a dream on his way home to the Old House that night. He had never imagined, never hoped that Ginevra could love him as a husband. She had refused his beautiful friend Donal the poet, and to himself Gibbie was much less, still only a burning heart running about in tattered clothing. The love that dwells in one man is an angel, the love in another is a bird, that in another is a hog. Gibbie's love was so unselfish that it asked for no return and also asked for no recognition; its existence didn't even have to be known. The desire to be loved is like a shadow cast by love, and Gibbie's love had no such shadow. Yet suddenly it was returned. All the other happiness in the city that night, added together, was not so much as Gibbie's happiness.

As he entered the courtyard of the Old House, Gibbie looked up. The windows of Mistress Croale's bedroom were glaring with light. He dashed up the stairs, smelling smoke. In Mistress Croale's room he found the curtains flaming to the ceiling. He tore them down and trampled on them. He threw the bedcovers over the flaming rags to try to smother the blaze. His hands were burned, but he hardly noticed.

Just then he heard a groan from the foot of the bed. Mistress Croale lay on her back on the floor with a red swollen face, her mouth wide open, her eyes half open—dead drunk. On one side of her lay a bottle, on the other side a fallen candelabra that had apparently started the blaze.

With the help of water from his own room he finally succeeded in putting out the fire, then turned his attention to Mistress Croale. Her breathing sounded so choked that he was alarmed and bathed her head. It was a strange   picture: the middle of the night, the fire-damaged room, the ugly female carcass on the floor, and the sad but somehow radiant young man watching her.

When gray morning came Mistress Croale stirred, slowly sat up, yawned and painfully stretched. Then she saw Gibbie and absolute terror distorted her bloated face. She stared at him and at the room like one who suddenly woke up in hell.

He lifted her up, put her cloak and bonnet on her, and led her out of the house. Sometimes her knees gave way, but Gibbie was an expert at helping people to walk home when they were unsteady. He brought her safely to her dingy little old room, which was exactly as she had left it. He had been paying the rent in case this happened. As soon as he left her there she fell on her bed and slept again.

She awakened from a terrible nightmare in which she was burning up, body and soul. As she lay there with her eyes closed thinking it over, she suddenly recalled that she had broken her promise to Gibbie. No wonder she had a headache and felt parched! She propped herself up on her elbow and opened her eyes. What a discovery! Her paradise was gone.

Gone was her respectability, friendship, honorable life, and chance to help the world. Her beautiful satin gown was a disgrace—wet, scorched, smeared with candle wax, smelling of smoke and whisky. Her lace was ruined.

After an hour of sitting on the edge of the bed in misery, she managed to cry some bitter tears and changed into an old cotton dress. On the table Gibbie had left her keys. Under them was a letter with five pounds in it and the message, "I promise to pay Mrs. Croale five pounds monthly, for nine months to come. Gilbert Galbraith." She wept again. She had lost him—her only friend—her only link to God and goodness and the kingdom of heaven.

She made a little fire and decided to take a jug to get water at the pump in the street. On the cupboard shelf by her water jug she saw her friend the black whisky bottle where she had left it. He had waited patiently all the time she was gone. She caught it up with a flash of fierce joy. One glass would free her from faintness, sickness, disgust. No one would find fault now or care what she did.

As she went to get a glass she saw Gibbie's loving and sorrowful face in her mind, looking like the face of Jesus. She turned, seized the bottle, and pushed the cork down into the neck. Then she put the bottle back on the shelf to serve as proof of victory some day. She would be strong and show Gibbie. A weaker person would have been foolish to keep whisky in the cupboard, but to her the constant reminder was a helpful challenge.

She hung her ruined satin gown near the cupboard as another reminder. Then she went out and got water and bread and butter and had tea and toast for supper.

In the morning she went back to work in her tiny shop. Her customers soon returned, and she refused to answer a word if they asked where she had been. The money from Gibbie and the fact that she wasted no more of her earnings on whisky allowed her to expand her business a little. In late autumn there was a time of disease and poverty in the city, and she went about helping the needy in a remarkable way. Gibbie heard about her good deeds, and his heart rejoiced.

She didn't see Gibbie. She watched for him like a lover, but this was a time of waiting, hoping, and working. She felt sure that when she asked him, he would forgive her.

60
GETTING READY

AFTER THE DREADFUL BRAWL neither Mr. Galbraith nor Fergus Duff guessed that Ginevra had left with Gibbie instead of going to her room. They had gathered what they could of their dignity and said good night to each other. When Mr. Sclater came to see the lord after breakfast the next morning, he was shocked to learn that Ginevra had spent the night in the Sclater home and not in her own bed.

"Send the hussy home instantly or I will come and get her," cried the outraged lord.

"She remains where she is. You want her to marry Fergus Duff and she prefers my ward, Gilbert Galbraith."

"She is under age," said her father.

"That will correct itself as fast in my house as in yours," returned the minister. "If you want the publicity of a court fight, I'll hire a lawyer."

"I am unspeakably shocked," the lord finally added. "For my daughter to leave the shelter of her father's house in the middle of the night—"

"At seven in the evening."

"And take refuge with strangers!" the lord continued.

"Friends, not strangers!" said the minister. "You hit her and drove her from your house, and you act shocked that she went to friends for help?"

"She has bad character!" fumed the lord.

"When a man is alone in his opinion, he is probably wrong," said Mr. Sclater. "Everyone except you admires Miss Galbraith."

By the time Mr. Sclater left, the lord had grudgingly promised not to try to force Ginevra into marriage to Fergus Duff. Gibbie was disappointed that she was returning home instead of marrying him immediately, but he understood the delay. Ginevra was in such high spirits now that she took her father's coldness and arrogance lightly. She said nothing when he praised Fergus and insulted Gibbie, because she knew time would change that. She was glad he still failed to realize that Gibbie owned Glashruach, because if he knew the truth he would turn against Fergus and want her to marry Gibbie for his property. That would be worse.

The lord confidently expected Gibbie to do something to disgrace himself and cause Ginevra to break the engagement. Fergus didn't even know about her engagement.

61

THE WEDDING

AT LAST FERGUS GRADUALLY CAME TO HIS SENSES and lost hope concerning Ginevra. He broke the news to her father that as much as he enjoyed their friendship, he would not come to visit much any more because Ginevra did not welcome his presence. The lord blustered against his daughter and insisted that she would decide to accept Fergus if he didn't give up too soon, but Fergus was no longer fooled. When he saw that Fergus was really leaving him, the lord made some acid remarks about Fergus being only a lowly farmer's son he had stooped to befriend. Fergus left, never to return.

There had lately come to Fergus's church a rich retired merchant with one daughter. She had money and good looks, and her father was respected although he was a nobody compared to the lord of Glashruach. Fergus saw that the honor of being Thomas Galbraith's son-in-law was not without serious drawbacks he hadn't considered. Within three months, Fergus courted and married Miss Lapraik and thought himself happy. He took to writing hymns as well as preaching and enjoyed fame, good health, a devoted wife, and full assurance that he was a great man.

Night after night the lord fidgeted, stormed, and sank into depression when Fergus did not come. He scorned Ginevra's offer to play backgammon, said she was too stupid to learn chess, and refused with contempt and sometimes absolute rage her offers to read to him. She feared that he was losing his mind.

When Gibbie returned from a visit to Glashruach, she told him how bad her father was, and they decided to go ahead and marry.

One morning Mr. Galbraith received a very polite letter from Mr. Torrie begging him respectfully to go to Glashruach to handle some papers for the new owner. If he agreed, a fine carriage with four horses would pick him up the next morning at ten. In his absolute boredom he was invigorated by this new chance to seem important, and he sent a note immediately saying he would go. He arranged for Miss Kimble to come to watch Ginevra.

At ten he got into the carriage with extreme stateliness and a fur coat on his arm, sensing his own personal grandeur. If he were not exactly lord of Glashruach again, he was something quite as important. Off he rode.

As soon as he left, another large carriage arrived to deposit Mr. and Mrs. Sclater, Sir Gibbie, and Mr. Torrie. Miss Kimble was bewildered as they trooped in. Four horses and a lawyer for a morning visit from the pastor? It must be religion, not business, because he promptly launched into Scripture and prayer. His words suddenly revealed to Miss Kimble that she was taking part in a secret wedding! There was Ginevra in a plain brown dress marrying that horrid creature. As soon as Mr. Sclater pronounced them man and wife, she shrieked, "I forbid it!" The only response she got was big smiles and soft laughter.

As Ginevra and Gibbie headed toward the carriage, she protested. Mr. Sclater told her that Ginevra was under no obligation to her at all. She wept in frustration, and Ginevra assured her they were setting out to overtake her father.

"A new kind of runaway marriage," Mr. Torrie laughed. "The happy couple are chasing the stubborn parent."

As soon as everyone was gone, Miss Kimble put on her bonnet and went to complain hotly to the minister Fergus Duff, who was sure to sympathize. He sighed and told himself it was a shame to see youth and beauty turn away from genius and respectability in order to marry money and idiocy instead.

The coach carrying the newlyweds passed the coach that carried Thomas Galbraith, and he never noticed it. When he arrived at Glashruach he saw that the approach was all changed and the grounds were rebuilt differently by the new owner, but he refused to take any interest. At the door a young woman—Donal's oldest sister, but of course he didn't know her—met him and took him up to his old study. His chair was by a cheerful fire, and wine and biscuits were waiting for him on a little table there. He made himself comfortable and dozed, dreaming of his dead wife.

In came Major Culsalmon with his wife, a hand stretched out in greeting. How young the major was. Oh, no! It was the half-witted impostor again! And that minx Ginny, smiling through tears. The dream of his wife must be continuing. He tried to wake up.

"Ginny, what is the meaning of this! Did Major Culsalmon invite you? What is this person doing here?"

"Papa, this is my husband Sir Gilbert Galbraith of Glashruach."

"Stop your foolishness. Inform Major Culsalmon that I request to see him immediately."

He cut her off by turning away and starting to read a newspaper. They left quietly, and by degrees the truth sank into his mind. Until the day of his death he never said another word about the matter. When dinner was announced, he took his old place at the table as if he had never left, but he didn't argue any more about who owned Glashruach.

The chest of family papers had been brought to Glashruach, and he busied himself in a study of them. He found that some of Gibbie's ancestors had lost property to Ginevra's ancestors, who seemed to have been dishonest lawyers. The transactions had amounted to swindling, a subject that interested Mr. Galbraith in more ways than one.

Studying the old papers and meddling with the affairs of the tenants, Mr. Galbraith lived on rather happily at Glashruach, half pretending that he was still the lord there.

62
THE CELEBRATION

EVERY WINTER FOR MANY YEARS Sir Gilbert and Lady Galbraith lived in the Old House in the city. What a change it was to Ginevra to help poor people in the city instead of living there as a prisoner! She found it difficult at first, of course. But help came. When Mistress Croale heard of their return, she went to Ginevra one day when Gibbie was at class and sank to her knees and wept and told the whole story, begging for Gibbie's friendship. The result was that she became his housekeeper again. In her remaining years she changed greatly for the better.

The Old House served as a refuge for all who could be helped there. Gibbie used caution and good common sense to keep this service for the truly needy who would not waste his efforts. A year later he built a house on Glashgar where invalids could spend the summer months under the care of Janet and her daughter Robina. Many grew strong enough there to earn a living again for a while afterwards.

As soon as the college term ended after their marriage, they returned to Glashruach. The lord, as he was still called, received them as if they were his guests. He had hired Joseph to be his butler—and Angus to be in charge of the animals. Ginevra warned Angus that they would tolerate him for her father's sake if he controlled himself, but that one violent act would result in his being fired and turned in to the sheriff. Donal's oldest brother was made sheriff. Gibbie soon settled three Grant brothers on one of his farms. Every Saturday so long as Janet lived, they all met at her cottage, but now Ginevra took Donal's place. Nicie came to work for Ginevra and be her friend. When she married, she and her husband stayed there.

Janet died first, as she had preferred. She wanted to be first, she used to say, "to be on hand to open the door to him when he knocks." Then Robert moved in with his sons on their farm until he died soon after.

But long before Janet and Robert went home (in their words), the changes in the great house were complete, and Gibbie celebrated with a dinner party for all the residents of Glashgar. Robert and Janet told him they were too old for making merry except in their own hearts, and that they would celebrate with him later in heaven. So Gibbie put Jean Favor in the place of honor as his special guest at the dinner. She was beside herself with joy to see her brownie the lord of the land. But her brother John Duff said it was clean ridiculous and believed Gibbie was a half-wit. He insisted that Ginevra did all the thinking and that Gibbie's finger-talk was a silly pretense that meant nothing. Thomas Galbraith avoided the dinner by pretending he had to go to the city on business that day, although he had no business any more.

When the main part of the dinner was over, Sir Gilbert and his lady made a little speech. He told of his adventures as a brownie, and his audience laughed until tears ran down their cheeks. Then he mentioned his strange childhood and thanked God for leading him into the very arms of love and peace in the cottage of Robert and Janet Grant. There, not in his wealth that came later, was his fortune.

The pair concluded by saying that when Sir Gilbert was a stranger the people of Daurside took him in, and he would always want to treat them kindly. Furthermore, he wanted them to know that a man born and bred among them, Donal Grant, had become a poet. That very morning a new poem had come from him in the mail, which Ginevra read aloud.

Afterwards, Sir Gilbert and Lady Galbraith walked over the enclosed bridge to the new part of the house. Ginevra looked out at the dry streambed as usual and sighed. She missed the song of the stream that had cheered her in her childhood. In spite of all the changes and restoration, her stream remained blocked by the landslip caused in the flood.

Gibbie opened the window and put a small pistol in her hand for her to fire up the dry channel. He laid his hand on hers to calm her trembling; she had never fired a gun. She pulled the trigger. The shot was a signal.

A roar followed a moment later, rolling from mountain to mountain. The next instant the landslip was in pieces, rushing down the rocky bed in mud-brown water. Roaring and leaping, the water shot under the bridge, back in its ancient course. The mud soon cleared away and a small mountain river, clear and sweet, was singing to them. Gibbie had planted gunpowder in the landslip and waited until now to detonate it as the final part of their celebration.

"Let's see it from my room, Gibbie!"

They went up to the turret window and looked down at the water until twilight darkened. They listened to its gentle sound.

"It's my own stream and its own singing," Ginevra said. "Gibbie, you give me everything."

"If I were the water, how I would run!" Gibbie sang, and Ginevra heard the words to Donal's first poem in her memory. She threw herself into her husband's arms and hid her face in his shoulder. Over her head he gazed out into the cool spring night, up the mountain to the stars. He felt as if he could have seen angels coming and going on Glashgar, but he didn't. Someone higher than angels was there with them.

Other books in the Young Reader's Library:

Black Beauty—Anna Sewell
Little Women (Books One and Two)—Louisa May Alcott
Robinson Crusoe—Daniel Defoe

About the author and *Sir Gibbie*

George Macdonald (1824–1905) was a Scottish novelist and poet whose works influenced such great writers as C. S. Lewis and G. K. Chesterton. Macdonald was the author of over fifty books, including novels, stories, and poems, and was one of the best-loved authors of his day. Among his better known children's stories, in addition to *Sir Gibbie* (written in 1879), are *At the Back of the North Wind* (1872) and *The Princess and the Goblin* (1872). He is acclaimed as one of the best storytellers of all time.

Macdonald's eldest son, Greville, wrote this about *Sir Gibbie:* "[It] is, I think, at once the most direct and most beautiful of all George Macdonald's novels. . . . Children . . . delight in its magic. . . ."

C. S. Lewis, writing to Arthur Greeves in 1930, also found *Sir Gibbie* to his liking: "[It] seems to me much better because the excitement in it is of the *real* sort. . . . Don't you love 'sleep was scattered all over the world'—and the lovely homeliness of the farm kitchen—and the apparition of Sir Gibbie when the old woman mistakes him for Christ?"

About the editor

Kathryn Lindskoog, an educator, literary critic, and expert on C. S. Lewis, authored more than twenty books, including *C. S. Lewis: Mere Christian, A Child's Garden of Christian Verses*, and *How to Grow a Young Reader.* She earned her B.A. at the University of Redlands and her M.A. at California State University at Long Beach. She taught as an adjunct instructor at Seattle Pacific University, Biola University, New Orleans Baptist Seminary, and Fuller Theological Seminary.

About the illustrator

Patrick Wynne has illustrated numerous books, including *Fish Soup* by Ursula K. Le Guin and *Light in the Shadowlands* by Kathryn Lindskoog. He was Artist Guest of Honor at Mythcon XXI in Long Beach, California, in 1990. He is an expert on J. R. R. Tolkien, serving as an editor of Tolkien's Gnomish and Qenya lexicons. Wynn lives in Fosston, Minnesota.